Criminally Spun Out

Book 5 of the Fiber Maven's Mysteries

By

J. Traveler Pelton

Potpourri Publishing, Limited
Mt. Vernon, OH 43050

COPYRIGHT

Criminally Spun Out: Book Five of the Fiber Maven's Mysteries by J. Traveler Pelton

Published in the U.S.A. by Potpourri Publishing
Cover design by RebecaCovers
Edited by Write Useful

Printed in the United States of America
First Edition published;
Books> fiction> cozy mystery
ISBN: 9798713190347

Dedication

First, to my God and Creator, Savior and Guide, who gives us dreams and tasks, who gifts us with imagination and who breathes life into our dreams. To my family who, while they do not possess infinite patience, are tolerant of the odd hours writers and other creative folks need to work. I love them all.

I dedicate with love to all those who have been to the shadowy edge of life, looked over and decided to come back and try again. I've been there, I came back; it was worth the fight. May you keep the warmth and wealth of love in your hearts always. Love is what keeps us whole.

I dedicate it to my ancestors who walked the Red Road before me. Someday we will all walk the Skylands together. Until then may our hearts beat with the drum of unity and peace.

May God grant us the courage to live with whatever life sends us and overcome trials always with His peace.

And to all fiber artists everywhere – you know who you are – that love a good mystery. May our tribe increase!

Finally, to my readers, because a story isn't a story until someone else hears it; it is simply a phantasm, a dream in the maker's head. You make it live when you read it and for just a few brief moments, our imaginations combine and that's when magic is still alive...

Other Books by Traveler Pelton
Spiritual Works
- <u>God Wanted to Write a Bestseller</u>
- <u>Big God, Little Me</u>
- <u>Lenten Stories for God's Little Children</u>
- <u>Natural Morning</u>
- <u>Ninety Days to The God Habit</u>
- <u>Tales for Advent and Christmas</u>
- <u>His Path Is Mine</u>
- <u>Calming my Clamor</u>
- <u>Calm Instead of Clamor</u>

Christian Literary Historical/Science Fiction

The First Oberllyn Family Trilogy: The Past
- <u>The Oberllyn's Overland: 1855-1862</u>
- <u>Terrorists, Traitors and Spies 1900-1990</u>
- <u>Rebooting the Oberllyn's 2015-2020</u>

The Second Oberllyn Family Trilogy: The Present
- <u>The Infant Conspiracy</u>
- <u>Kai Dante's Stratagem</u>
- <u>The Obligation of Being Oberllyn</u>

The Third Oberllyn Family Trilogy: The Future
- <u>To Protect One's Own</u>
- <u>The Importance of Family Ties</u>
- <u>Kith and Kin, Together Again</u>

- <u>The First Oberllyn Family Omnibus</u>
- <u>The Second Oberllyn Family</u>
- <u>The Third Oberllyn Omnibus</u>

The Fiber Mavens Mystery Series
- Quilting Can be Criminal
- Criminally Quilted
- Criminally Pieced Together
- Criminally Crocheted
- Criminally Spun Out

In Collaboration with T. Bear Pelton:
- Clan Falconer's War
- The Rise of the Rebellion
- Changeling's Clan
- Forged in Water and Fire

Other Authors Associated with Potpourri Publishing

Lynette Spencer of Write Useful
- Sewing on a Budget
- Vegetarian Cooking on a Budget

Dan Pelton
- The Majestic Spectrum of God's Love

Chapter One

The doorbell chimed as a woman entered the Fiber Avalanche, carrying a large bag of what appeared to be fiber. Lydia met her as she headed back for the store checkout.

"Good morning!" Lydia smiled. "Lovely day out, yah? May I help you?"

"For a chilly fall day, it's lovely out," smiled the stranger. "Is Allyssa here? I have a one o'clock appointment with her."

"Welcome!" exclaimed Allyssa from the top of a ladder. She was putting up fall displays near the right side of the store. "You must be Dana. Lydia, this is our new spinning instructor."

"Spinning instructor?" asked Lydia. "I thought she wasn't coming until next week?"

"The class starts next week. I asked her to come in and get acquainted today with us and the store. Can you fetch over my sister and as many of the rest of the staff as are available so she can get to know us all? We'll just go back to the meeting room. Clarissa, can you watch the register?"

"Yes, ma'am," answered a young lady getting down from her step stool. She had been putting yarn into cubbyholes. She looked at the newcomer, tilted her head, and asked "Do you have one of those folding spinning wheels in that bag? I've always wanted to see one."

Dana grinned. "Oh, no, just fiber I wanted to share and figure out where to hang."

"Yes, we'll be carrying her yarns and fiber roving once she gets started properly," Allyssa smiled as she came down the ladder, pushing her hair back into its bun and straightening her apron. "Are Thom and Mike here?"

"Coming wife," called out Mike. "New staff? We got champagne?"

"You'll have to do with tea," laughed his wife.

"Long as it's that peppermint cocoa kind you got last week. Stuff is really tasty."

The Fiber Mavens shop was owned and operated by Allyssa Martin and her Amish helper Lydia Fisher; with the assistance of seasonal help Clarissa Jacobs and Annie Malcom. It formed the center of a block-wide, all-in-one-building craft mall. Fabric Avalanche quilt shop owner Suzanne Hays, Allyssa's sister, and her helper Miriam Miller ran the only fabric store in town, and Clarissa and Annie worked between the two stores, which were open to each other, helping whichever side needed them the most. Thom's Hobbies adjoined his wife Suzanne's shop and catered to the RC hobbyists in the town. Not Your Normal Antique Store adjoined Fiber Mavens and was run by Mike Martin and his son Alan. The Yarn Sisters, an eclectic group of ladies of all ages, from Casey Malcom's twin babies to eighty-three-year-old Sophia Drummel, met weekly in the meeting room, making projects, gossiping, eating goodies, and having a high old time. The Oldtimers RC club met once a week in Thom's store and had been known to wander over to the Yarn Sisters to filch cookies. They'd rearranged their own meeting to coincide with the ladies' get together to sneak over at half-time, as Thom was wont to say. The ladies just shook their heads, knowing that the menfolk would show up for work bees if needed as long as they kept them fed.

Everyone worked together and the big old store, with four apartments on the second floor, was a hive of activity most days and a flagship of the local tourist trade. All in one place, a lady could bring her husband and he stay happily lost while she went yarn stashing or fabric browsing. Neither would bother the other with what they got because both would most likely be guilty of some splurge buying. Thom was fond of saying if you couldn't find it in one of their stores, it didn't need found. Not Your Normal Antique Store included a small private museum of not-for-sale items that Mike regularly rotated and it fascinated just about anyone, and if a person weren't crafty, they'd still find things to look at and pass the time with while the rest of the family picked out to-die-for yarns and fabrics.

Dana was led to the staff room in the far back where the water was hot, the tea tray ready and a plate of cookies and small sandwiches waited.

"Everyone, listen up," announced Allyssa. "When we rearranged the store this spring to give us more room, you all noticed I left one corner section nearly empty and I told you it was for expansion into more fiber arts. I wanted to be able to allow the folks in our town to have total control over their fiber projects. Short of buying a herd, we can stock roving and wheels for them so they can learn to make their own yarn, and then take a dying class to get it the right color without harming the fiber and then take it to a crocheting or knitting class and bring it to the finished project and be able to say they did it all."

"Short of having animals themselves," mused Thom. "I like that. Total control over your art."

"Yes, and I've been looking for just the right teacher. I met Dana at the Yarn Expo two months ago. She had wonderful rovings and was giving a demonstration on how to spin and the audience loved her. I asked her about traveling to give some classes and the funny thing was she told me she was moving shortly. I asked her where and it turns out this way. She's even a judge of roving and fleeces at fiber shows. She bought that little farm out there next to Casey. I asked her to take time out of moving in to come to meet us all and let us see some of the products she'll be adding to our store. Dana? Would you tell us a little about yourself?"

"I'd be pleased to!" she started, sitting down her tea. "I've been spinning since I was nine years old. I learned from my mom and her mom. My mom and I bought that little twenty-acre place out on Painter Road six months ago, and we've had men out there painting and repairing and fixing the fences and such for us. We've been moving into it now, finally, and so far it's fitting us well. My animals will be arriving tomorrow. I raise alpaca, highland cattle, pyagora goats, angora rabbits, Southdown sheep, and Mom has canaries. I mean a lot of canaries. We have one entire room on the sunny side of the house set up for her birds alone. It's a lovely old farmhouse, so the two of us have plenty of room for our businesses. I shear my animals in the spring, and I pluck the rabbits in the summer and I use their fleeces to spin. I have contacts just about everywhere to get the other fleeces I need for my work: merino and yak, camel and mohair, silk, bamboo, and even some dog hair. We've got a grand barn with space for my animals at one end and hay storage overhead. We have closed off half of the upper and lower floor for my fiber work; we added windows for light and it's a lovely studio. I have my looms, my wheels, my dying vats, everything on the first floor, and all the storage for my business and my office on the second. Most of my work I sell online and at shows and branching into putting it in stores is exciting."

She took a sip of her tea. "That chocolate mint tea is great. Anyway, I brought some samples here of things I do, with the help of my mom who lives with me and sometimes my daughters, but they're off to university and aren't home as much as they used to be." She pulled out various plastic bags and a couple of boxes. "In these boxes are drop spindles I've collected in my travels, marked with the countries I got them in and the kind they are. The longest one is this Dineh one used to spin wool for blankets. It's almost a meter long. The smallest is this one that's really portable since it's only 8 inches long and made with one of those 3-d printers. I got it at a tech show with my hubby two years ago."

She took a deep breath. "He and my son were killed in a plane accident a year ago coming back from a mission trip and I still miss them a lot. It's one of the reasons I sold out where we lived and moved here, into the countryside. We were sort of cramped where we lived before, having just six acres, and now we can expand and be busy and put away some of the old memories. My mom is also a widow, although my dad died years ago. She's a bird person; she judges bird shows and has an entire trophy case of awards for having the best singers and all that. She has around three hundred canaries, I think. They're quite vociferous so they have the entire top floor along with mom at the farmhouse. At any rate, I have almost a hundred different spindles now. I have a Great wheel, also called a walking wheel, one I got from a small museum that was going out of business. If I believe the provenance, it dates from the late fifteen hundreds. It still works. I have a seventeenth century Saxon wheel and several others in my collection. I personally like my magicraft rose wheel for my own art spinning. The rovings I've brought are ones I either raised from my own animals, or obtained from friends."

She opened the big purse and started handing out small bags with roving samples. "These bags are let's see, camel, and yak and mugo silk from India – see it's gorgeous gold color? It was reserved for royalty. It's like spinning gold."

"Sort of like the original Rumpelstiltskin?" asked Thom, touching the fiber.

"Absolutely. And this is bamboo, and these are various yarns I've spun. My skeins are all 220 yards, which is standard and I make mostly worsted or sports weights. I dye it with natural dyes in most cases. I want to get my dye garden in this coming spring; I've collected the seeds and such from the beds I had back in Indiana and hope they'll do well. There are already some of the trees and bushes I would use on the farm and I feel fortunate about that. I teach classes in spinning with drop spindles and with wheels and dying your own fiber. I sell entire fleeces to some folks – the same lady every year buys Herman's fleece as soon as he's shorn, she likes the feel of that alpaca so much."

The ladies all but cuddled the rovings and yarns. "These are so soft!" exclaimed Lydia. "I can see it for a baby sweater."

"That's cria roving. A cria is a baby alpaca. This is merino, bamboo, and silk," said Dana, pointing at a different ball of roving. "And I do use it for baby things."

"And the colors are just lovely," said Suzanne. "These blended ones are simply incredible, look at this one, black, yellow, white, a touch of blue"

"That's called chickadee," smiled Dana. "I was thinking of the little bird when I made it. It spins up into a variegated yarn, like this." She showed them a ball of yarn. "I also make up beginning kits that have a drop spindle; I normally use ones made by some of my craft friends because I like to support my fellow craft folks. I've brought some stock in the truck if you want to put up a display ahead of the class."

"That is exactly what I want to do!" exclaimed Allyssa. "Thom and Mike, can you help her carry it all in? Dana, we'll get your paperwork done as one of our consigners, and help you get things set up for people to sign up for the class. Mildred Carmichael left us four spinning wheels we thought we could use for classes, and there are some drop spindles."

"Are you planning on selling the wheels?" asked Dana.

"No, I want to keep them here for our people to use."

"Fine. Let's get my things in, where ever it is you want them to go and get the display up, and then let me see your wheels and such so I can be certain they'll work. Oh, and I also weave, not as good as my mom who is a master weaver and might be induced, later when she gets used to folks, to give weaving lessons."

"Really? That would be tremendous!" exclaimed Suzanne. "But looms are so expensive."

"Not if you start with small lap looms. You can get a small, flat lap loom for under thirty dollars; the larger ones are fifty, and move into a tapestry loom or onto a rigid heddle loom for under three hundred. The bigger floor models can get pricey but by the time you work up to them, you're ready for that sort of investment. But one thing at a time," said Dana. "From my experience, you want to be continuously rolling out something new every six months or so in a logical progression to make the most out of it."

"Did you have a store?" asked Mike.

"My mom and grandma did, I sell at fiber shows mostly and teach at other's stores. Running an actual store is way too time intensive and takes away from my art. I do have an online shop my mom tends. I have several YouTube videos out. I care for our animals, shear and prepare the fleeces for the mill, make the yarn, dye the yarn and teach classes. And most the time, we're way too busy to be lonesome."

"I don't suppose you'd allow me to exhibit these drop spindles at the Museum for a couple of weeks, would you?" asked Mike. "I have a locked case they can go into and I know a lot of people would be interested in them. I think it would build interest in your class as well."

"I'd like to see all of your stores when we're done with the set-up," said Dana. "I think this is going to be fun. Let's talk about displays after we're done with one thing. Oh! Nearly forgot. It's getting cold out and I brought each of you a scarf woven of alpaca, angora, and silk. I brought eight of them, and they're different colors and weaves, so if you could all pick one?"

"You didn't have to do that!" exclaimed Allyssa, petting the pile of scarves Dana held out.

"This is exquisite," said Suzanne, rubbing one against her cheek. "I may not want to take it off. Feel the nap and the softness!"

Mike wrapped his around his neck. "It's not scratchy. I hate scratchy. This doesn't itch at all."

"Mike's sensitivities to wools are just about legendary around here," said Allyssa. "Get him near some real sheep's wool even in a blend and, boom, hives all over. That he's not reacting to this alpaca is grand."

"Now here's one for that young lady who was out at the cash register trying to mind it all? What's her favorite color?"

"Clarissa's favorite color is green, so let me take this one to her. And guys, bring in Dana's stuff to the display corner I set up for her. We all need to get back to work. This is simply so exciting."

Chapter Two

For the next few hours, boxes were carried in and unpacked or stored, paperwork was accomplished, and a general tour of the four stores and a map of the town produced so Dana and her mom could find everything; by the end of the morning, Dana blew out a gasp and nodded her head in satisfaction.

"You have a great set-up here!" she exclaimed. "I am going to be so glad to be part of it. I have to get back home soon and help Mom finish unpacking her cages so we can settle the canaries into their new aviaries and a guy is coming with hay later."

"Well, here's a set of all the other classes we're running this month; and we thought if your first one could start next Thursday night, it would fit in," replied Allyssa.

"Thank you! I'll get this all entered into the computer when I get back home. Let me just finish a few things here in the corner."

Dana had agreed to allow Mike to put her drop spindles on display in the museum case. Mike took the mummified cat and pipe collection out of the locked glass cabinet right by the cash register and settled the drop spindles into the display on green velvet, using the labels Dana had already provided. He looked at it in satisfaction. "I'll just feature it in my email newsletter tomorrow," he said to himself, "A lot of ladies are going to want to see these."

The newest display in the Fiber Mavens Shop had a banner displayed across the top proudly calling it The Spinner's Corner. It had two pegboard walls with bags of fiber and already spun yarns matching the fibers next to it. It had small baskets of each kind of fiber so people could feel before they bought, and it had basic spinning needs, a jar of drop spindles of differing colors, sizes, weights, and types, several small books, a scale with a bowl to weigh out roving. There were also hanging small bag kits for beginners and small bags of natural dyes. Three sign-up sheets were set up for different types of spinning: drop spinning, wheel spinning, and blending. A carder and a spinning wheel were displayed. The ladies all stood back and studied the display.

"There! Not too much, not too little, I think it's good. I really like that little bio there with the picture of you and your herd. They're sweet!"

"That was taken last spring," Dana told her. "I think my animals were all that kept my head on after the accident. Speaking of which I've got to get back. I have a load of hay being brought in at 5 this afternoon, and I need to get it all stored safely and the canaries in their flights with Mom all before supper."

"Then we'll see you next Thursday for the first class."

"I hope we have enough sign up to make it worth your while," fretted Dana. "A week is not long to gather students."

"I already have three people for the beginner's class," Allyssa replied. "You're capping it at 10."

"It's better that way. I can give them individual help. We'll use drop spindles to start and I have plenty of those. Thanks for your help."

"Thank you for coming. Have a safe trip home."

Deputy Jed came into the shop.

"Afternoon, welcome!" said Allyssa. "You on business, Jed?"

"Wife said she needs," he pulled out a three-by-five card and read off of it. "She needs two more skeins of that blue yarn she bought Thursday. And wants to know if she can sign up for the spinning class. Is that some sort of biking thing? She was complaining about her baby weight."

Lydia broke into a fit of giggles and left to get the yarn and write Jed's wife's name on the sign-up sheet. She pulled out the handout about the spinning class, Jed paid for the yarn and the class and left.

Lydia and the other ladies went back to what they were doing before Dana came that morning and shortly it was time to close up and go home.

Chapter Three

"There, there, honey, I know it's nasty tasting, but it will help," Casey crooned to Kai as she rubbed teething medicine on his gums. He sniffed and fussed. She handed him a frozen teether and went to help little one-year-old Enya, his twin sister, with the same medicine. She didn't like it any better than her brother. Casey snuggled them both into their swings and started the timer and soft music. The sniffly babies sobbed softly before dropping off for a nap.

Casey sighed. "Gracious, I hate teething. At least while they're asleep, I can get the kitchen cleaned up and the dinner in the oven, and I might be able to dictate those notes. Best get running, but boy, could I use a nap!"

Casey slammed through the kitchen like a grasshopper, dashing from one area to another, bringing organization out of chaos. Just as she put a casserole in the oven, the back door opened and in stepped Brad, her husband.

"Hi, honey, how are the kids?" He said as he stepped up and kissed her. "Don't worry, not hungry, ate lunch already at the office during a meeting."

"Teething. To what do I owe the honor of your presence in the middle of the day?"

"Appears some youngsters on rumspringa may have screwed up and I'm heading over to talk to them and their dads."

"Oh? They usually keep a hat on everything."

"I know. This time, a bit more mischief than needed. Got them dead to rights on a security camera by the fire department setting off firecrackers. Marsha Downing sent me a copy of the tape. She's sort of steamed so I guess I have to visit two dads."

"They don't like photos."

"I know, but these boys haven't joined church yet. Their dads are reasonable. Marsha said she was coming over this afternoon?"

"Yes, I need to run into the office for some sessions between 2 and 5; supper's in the oven and will be ready by then. I'll get home at 5:30, put it all on the table in time for you to show up at 6. Annie will take over for Marsha at 4, so hopefully the babies won't be too upset with me not being here."

"Well, Marsha's an EMT so I suspect she'll know how to cope with teething. Anyway, stopped by to get a kiss, grab a bottle of soda, and I'm off. Where's Rutherford? He likes to ride along."

"He was on the back porch."

Brad had walked to the living room to peek at his twins and grinned. "Nah; he's on duty."

"What?" Casey came to look around him.

Rutherford had stretched his huge frame across the front of the baby swings and was lying there, alert. He heard Brad, looked at him, but didn't bark. His very attitude said nobody better come close to these two puppies or they'd contend with him. He sat up and nudged the left swing to keep it rocking back and forth and then he lay back down.

"Hey, old man, I need you on a run," said Brad. Rutherford sat up and looked at the babies, shook his head and stood up, yawned widely, and came over to his master. He looked back at the puppy twins and then at Casey as if to tell her they'd better be right there when he returned. She laughed softly, petted the dog, and went back to her work.

Rutherford got into the back seat of the patrol car and Brad headed out into the countryside to talk to three errant Amish teens, smiling to himself as he drove. "I live in the best place on God's green earth and I have the prettiest wife and best children in the world. It cannot get better than this, Lord, and I thank you for my blessings."

Suddenly, from the back seat, Rutherford growled and then barked, He sat up and started pawing at the door.

"What's up, old man? You see something?"

Brad pulled the car over to the side of the road and onto a small field driveway. He got out and let Rutherford out. Rutherford ran into the field and stood barking next to an idled tractor.

A man was lying by the wheel, barely conscious. Brad radioed for an ambulance.

"Brad?" whispered the man. "Careful, I got hit with 'bout a thousand hornets cleaning up this field. Ought not to be any hornets out here. Got dizzy trying to get away, fell off the tractor."

"Ambulance is on the way. Who's at home, Carl?"

"Wife is home. Phone out of power so I couldn't call. I feel like I've been out here hours, but maybe not."

Rutherford ran back to the squad car and brought back the emergency bag Brad always carried in the front. Brad took out water and held it as Carl took some swallows.

"Man, that's good. I'm so thirsty." Brad checked his pulse, and it was missing beats. There were large welts all over the man's head and face, hands, and Brad guessed all over his torso.

"Sip it slow. Once the ambulance is here, I'll run over and let your wife know."

"I think Rutherford may already have taken off for that." Rutherford was streaking across the field and came back barking.

Just then, Brad's radio went off.

"Detective Malcom. There is a 10-70 at the Hershberger farm. Units dispatched. Give help if possible. What's your status?"

"Roger that, I have an ambulance on the way here with a farm injury: I can go over if needed."

"Negative. I'll dispatch Jed and Danny over to see if the fire department needs help."

"You busy today?" gasped Carl.

"Seems like. Here's the ambulance, Rutherford's going to lead them right here."

Rutherford ran between the EMT's and Brad, urging hurry. The men came over and started caring for Carl.

"I'll head over to the house and let your wife know. You guys need anything?" asked Brad.

"Got it covered, Officer," said one. "My gosh, looks like you've been hit way more than twenty or thirty times, Carl. We're taking you into emergency. I'll get the stretcher."

Brad and Rutherford made their way to the car, Rutherford kept lifting his muzzle and whining. "Yeah, I smell it too. Looks like Hershberger's farm. We had to stop there anyway, so let's just mosey over. You stay in the car, old fella. Hate to lose you trying to rescue somebody from a fire."

Carl's wife took off her apron, grabbed her purse, and headed into the emergency room as soon as the detective had given his message. She thanked Brad and drove out behind him, turning left as he turned right.

At Hershberger's, fifty Amish men were lined up throwing water at the barn, which was burning. The pumper truck was pouring water on it as well.

"The stock is safe," said David Hershberger. "Hay is a total loss. There was no storm, and the hay was good and dry, I just don't see how we could have had a fire. If it hadn't been for your dog barking like that, we'd not have looked up and seen smoke and we'd have lost our stock."

"Really?"

"I could hear Rutherford all across the field – we were finishing up digging potatoes and I heard him bark," said David's oldest boy. "He's got that big low voice and I looked over to see what he was barking about and I saw the smoke over the barn and we ran back. By the time we got here, I heard some pops and the barn went up. I hit the gong and ran inside to lead out the horses, and the cattle stampeded out. We may have lost a few chickens but not much else."

Brad frowned. "Fire Marshall will look it over," he informed them, "Anyone hurt?" The men shook their heads and started to go back to fight the fire, but Brad called Hershberger back. "By the way, I know this is a bad time, but where is your boy Ezekiel?"

"He's in the line helping with the water," answered David. "Why? Is he in trouble I don't know about? He got a burn on his hand but had to help."

Brad looked at his feet a moment. He sighed. "I have to show you something." He pulled out a photo of Ezekiel, Levi, and Joshua at the firehouse, setting off fireworks in the dark until they were chased off.

"You wouldn't maybe have some fireworks leftover from July 4?"

David was frowning as was his oldest son. "You think they had fireworks stored in the barn and that caused this fire?"

"It's possible. I don't want to cause you more upset than is already happening but I do need to question him. I know he's just turned 16 and is doing the rumspringa thing but it has to be done safely. Fireworks are against the law."

"And he may have burned down our barn." David cupped his hands around his mouth and called out, "Ezekiel

Hershberger. Here, now." A young man looked up, saw the officer with his dad, and seemed to wilt. He handed off his bucket. His oldest brother came over and took his place so the water could keep its steady stream.

"Ezekiel, where were you when this picture was being taken of you?" demanded his father. Ezekiel looked at the small video without comment at first. "Me and the guys were just fooling around. We weren't hurting anyone."

"Did you know it's illegal to shoot fireworks off in the city limits?" asked Brad.

"Well, no. But there's that concrete pad and we figured if we fired them off there behind the firehouse, it would be safer than out here in the field where it's dry now."

"So, the cement pad behind the firehouse would be safer, right in the center of town where there are literally hundreds of people trying to sleep, in wooden houses that could catch fire in this dry spell rather out here in the fields where all you'll burn up is grass??" asked Brad.

"That was our reckoning, I guess." He shuffled his feet. "I guess we're in trouble. I didn't know that lady inside had a camera."

Brad sighed. "There are security cameras all over town and you and the guys were caught on several of them."

"Did you have the fireworks stored in the barn?" demanded his father.

"I only had some cherry bombs left and yah, they were in the barn. But there wasn't anybody in there shooting them off. I had them in one of the feed bins."

"How old were they?" asked Brad.

"They were left over from a couple of years ago. We found them and so I don't know."

"Did you know those old firecrackers can go unstable and shoot off by themselves? Your older brother heard some pops as he ran across the field to save the stock. How many were there?"

Just then, there was a sound of a string of fireworks in the barn. The men all jumped and backed up as if a gun had gone off.

Brad ran over to the men calling out, "It's ok, there were some firecrackers in the barn, not ammunition. Keep working!" The men went back to pouring water on the remaining structure.

The fire chief came over. "This one of the boys who had the crackers at the fire station last night?" Brad nodded. Ezekiel looked glum and David looked like a trip to the woodshed was in order, right now.

"I'll be visiting the other two boys at their homes."

"They're here, helping put out the fire with their families," said David. "There's Levi and Joshua together in the bucket line. I'll just go get them and their dads."

The fire was coming under control. The fire chief turned to Brad. "Thanks to that loudmouthed dog of yours, the fire was noticed in time to avoid losing the entire barn, but their hay is ruined, back wall will need replaced, some of the roof. It could have been a lot worse. At least, no human or stock injuries. Won't take them long to repair and rebuild, I suspect one good work bee might do it."

"It's too bad it had to happen," remarked Brad as two Amish fathers and two ashamed boys came over. Brad thought he had a long afternoon ahead of him, working out the mess.

Just then. Mrs. Hershberger came up with a puzzled expression on her face and a pitcher of lemonade in her hand. Her daughter was with her with a tray of cookies and tin cups.

"Thank you so much for coming to help," she began. She offered them each a cup of cold lemonade and a cookie. "I found something odd though, on my way out the back door."

"What's that, ma'am?" asked Brad. "You surely make the best peanut butter cookies."

"I found this stuck in the screen on the back porch. It's one of those drop spindle things, isn't it?"

Brad took it and looked it over. "I take it you don't anyone here spin yarn?"

"No, we do not. I wouldn't know where it came from. And why would they stick it through the screen?" Brad put it in an evidence bag. "Was there a note or anything?"

She shook her head. "No, it was just hanging there. I'll have the boy repair the screen for me this afternoon so flies can't come in to plague us. I'm going to go get refreshments out on the table for folks." The women left. A picnic table was being covered with sandwiches and cold drinks, cookies and a pie.

The fire was out. Brad told each of the boys they'd have to go in front of a judge, but for now could stay in their homes. They had to consider themselves on house arrest, meaning not to go anywhere, just do their chores and stay home. Their fathers agreed.

As Brad turned to go, Joshua came up to him. "Mr. Malcom, I am sorry for what we did. We did not mean to start a fire. It was a dumb thing to do."

"Where exactly did you find those firecrackers?" asked Brad.

Joshua looked surprised. "We didn't exactly find them. An older lady gave them to us. She said she was cleaning out her basement and found them and thought we might like to go shoot them off. It did seem a little odd; she was just walking with them in her purse and saw me at my uncle's woodshop. She came to where I was stacking slab wood and gifted me with them. They were in a plastic bag. I thanked her and she went inside the store and bought, I think, a wooden bowl from my uncle."

"Do you know who she was?"

Joshua shook his head. "She was just an old lady. I don't recall seeing her before. I need to get over and join my father and brothers." He nodded and went over to the table.

Brad watched him go and then turned to his car. "I got the feeling, Rutherford, some boys are going to have a hard time sitting down tonight. Odd how their stories don't match. They all agreed they shot off the fireworks, but not how they got them in the first place. Wonder why Zeke would lie about it, unless he knows the old lady in question. Just being heedless and foolish, I guess. Good thing the barn wasn't a total loss. Let's get home. Casey will be wondering where we are."

Chapter Four

Toby pushed back his chair and sighed. "You know, you ladies do all of this so much better than I do. You sure you want me helping?"

Helen laughed. "Oh, you aren't going to get out of it that easily," she said. "It's your wedding too."

"But everything I suggest gets vetoed."

"Not everything. You wanted a November wedding and we've got a date for that."

"But you don't like the idea of orange and yellow tablecloths and dying the cookies to match them."

"We aren't having cookies, one, I hate orange, two, and where in the world did you ever come up with that idea of the food matching the tablecloths?"

"Well, it looked good on you tube. I remember it being like mint green and pink and I don't like pink, so why not fall colors?"

Marti Clamons, his sister-in-law, Toby's wife-to-be Helen, Jane Long from the Getaway Café, and the pastor's wife Sally were making wedding plans. Helen, being the organized person she was, had set up the wedding/reception committee to help her, and, so far things were working out pretty well. They had gotten the church date set up, the pastor set up, the musicians set up, and were now going into the sorts of details that generally drive men bats.

"Ok, so we are having the cake made by Hannah, Matthew Armstrong is the best man, and Troy, Kevin, and Dave are the groomsmen. Marti is Matron of Honor, and Annie,

Megan, and Sharon are bridesmaids. Troy's little girl Betsy is flower girl and Billy is ringbearer. The wedding colors are going to be burgundy and gold. We're going to use those pretty lights the church already has, and that adorable arbor and the candelabra, with the little kerosene lanterns in the windows, and Millie over at the flower shop is doing the flowers. Have the men got their tuxes lined up?" asked the bride.

"With burgundy cummerbunds," replied Toby. "Ricci is going to do the reception dinner catering and the rehearsal dinner is going to be at the Cafe. We're covered for food, place, clothes, and personnel. Can't be much more, right?"

"We have the invitations left to mail. I and my friends got them all addressed and wondered if you could take them to the post office tomorrow and send them out. Oh, and that photographer from Millersburg has the date clear and is coming for pictures."

"Sure, I can mail them. How many are we inviting?" he asked as he eyed the stacks of envelopes. "In fact, why don't I run over now to mail them? Why are they rubber banded together?"

"I organized them into invitations for here in town, in the county, in the state, and then out of state. We're inviting just a little over 300, but I don't think they'll all come."

"If we do, is there enough room?"

"I included info on the local bed and breakfasts if they want to stay over for the out of staters, and the sanctuary seats five hundred. Oh, and I arranged for the nursery to be manned so we ought not have any crying infants."

Toby sighed as he loaded up the card box with the prepared envelopes and stood up. "What else needs done?"

"Right now, we just let this stuff all percolate; we allow everyone to do their parts and the bridesmaids and bride go for dress fittings. I suggest you keep me posted," replied Sally. "It's going to be lovely. Have you decided where you're going on honeymoon?"

"He has but he won't tell me," exclaimed Helen, playfully hitting her fiancé in the shoulder. "But my son Sky is going to be with his grandpa for a week."

"You'll like where we go. It's pretty there."

"I suspect it is. Thank you, everyone, for meeting with us."

"No worries." said Sally as she gave Helen a hug. "You and John have your last prenuptial session next Wednesday at 6, don't forget. Then six more weeks and it's wedding bells for you guys!"

Sally led them out of the side door of the parsonage to their waiting cars. She waved as they left and went inside to her own chores. "I so do love weddings," she mused as she worked on the laundry. "All that hope and all those dreams all tied into a bundle and settled on the couple's hearts. I hope they stay tied tight their whole lives."

Chapter Five

Alan stood up and stretched. He went over and gave his mom, Allyssa, hug. "Meeting the new vet today, Mom. She's meeting me over at the old Malec place out on Painter Road. The new owner has fixed it up and she has a load of animals coming today and wants a vet on hand to be sure they're all healthy as we unload them. I have no idea how long I'll be or what I'm doing but it's going to be fun." He grinned at his mom. "I'm really glad to get this summer internship with the vet. It will help me get into vet school."

"Well, finishing your freshman year of college in high school helped, and being able to get the next two years credits in by working hard put you up ahead of the other guys applying for space in the program. Your grades are great and you deserve some fun time off. You went four full quarters in a row and I'm glad this summer you're doing some hands on."

"I'm going to enjoy working with the new vet. She does both large and small animals and even some exotics." He chugged down a glass of milk. "I really look forward to the exotics."

His mom stood still a moment as if in thought. "You said Painter Road? Our new spinning instructor bought the old farm on Painter Road. You'll get to meet her animals before I do."

"Any idea what?" he asked as he snagged a banana and peeled it.

"She said alpaca, some sort of small cow, sheep, rabbits, and … canaries, was it? I think so. Lots of canaries."

"No snakes or lizards? That's probably good. I've done some reading on the cows and sheep so I might be able to keep up a little."

"Best be on your way. You don't want to be late."

Taking the last bite of banana, Alan Martin headed out to his little Nissan truck. He'd earned the money for it himself; it was paid for and it ran reliably, although his dad thought it was held together more with bumper stickers and duct tape than metal. He'd replaced the seats, fixed the hole in the floor with metal he soldered in place, and covered the floor with rugs. The back had always had a cover on it, so the truck bed was good, and the new tires he'd just put on had set him back a little but he ought not have trouble driving to and from school this winter. Last winter had been a caution with those old tires. He planned on driving this truck until he graduated and one year after he got his practice up and running; then he'd buy a truck for his practice.

Alan was a cautious man about debt; he was careful and he hoped to leave school with little to none. He leaned back and drove out consistently smaller roads, heading out for Painter. The early summer scenery went by pretty much unheeded as he considered what the new vet might want of him. *Probably muscle*, he thought to himself. *Good thing I keep in shape.*

He pulled into the long drive and noted with approval the new fence that had replaced the old trampled one around the front fields. Looked like they'd replaced the house siding and some windows, and the barn was repaired and neatly painted white with black trim. It looked cared-for now, like a real home farm, like the one he'd dreamed about having for himself since he was a kid. All it needed was a good farm dog, a border collie or a Pyrenees. He made his way up the long drive and parked beside the vet's blue truck, which had a sign emblazoned on the side.

Amanda Zoland, DVM.
Pleasant Valley Vet Clinic, Carter Street
777-234-2368
Visit our webpage at Pleasant Valley AZ
or email us AtoZ@gmail.com

He nodded. Nicely businesslike. Carter Street, so she must have bought out the old vet who retired a year ago.

Amanda walked around the other side of the truck and over to him. "We're waiting for the truck to arrive; I've checked the cages and enclosures and she has a top-notch set-up here. I'm Dr. Zoland. You must be Alan?"

"Yes, ma'am. All ready to get started. What do you want me to do?"

"Here, you're a little big, but I think this will cover your clothes. For the future, you might want to get some of those coveralls they sell at the Farmer's Exchange or TSC. What we do can get dirty. You might not care, but unless you do your own laundry, I'm betting your mom will." She handed him a plain blue vet coat. It seemed to fit perfectly as he put it over his dark blue pocket tee and jeans.

"Are your hiking boots steel toed?" she inquired. "Might want to look into that as well. You haven't lived until a bull steps on your foot."

"I'll do that. Are there any bulls today?"

"One bull, one male sheep, a couple male alpaca, a couple gelded llamas and, if I understood her right on the phone, a camel or two."

"Camels?"

"I may be wrong on that last one. Might be goats. Last vet's records were handwritten and pretty poor. She has all their vet records and faxed me records, let's see." She rummaged through her phone. "We're going to unload them one at a time, update shots, give them a booster, check their temps, be sure they're thrifty, you know, no outward signs of bad health or possible problems, and then lead them to their places. Owner will be helping, and her mom. You're going into your senior undergrad?"

"Yes, ma'am and I'm sending in apps to five vet schools in January."

"Grades good?"

"Yes, ma'am."

"And I'm not old enough to be a ma'am, call me Dr. Zoland in front of clients, and Amanda when they aren't around. You going to try for OSU and Toledo?"

"And Findlay, Otterbein, and Kent. One of them has to like me."

She laughed. "You'll get some love, don't worry. Make sure you've got some experience – which if you stick with it this summer and next, you will – and good references and the financial aid lined up, and you'll do fine. Looks like the truck's coming."

"Where did you attend?" he asked as they watched the large stock truck pulling up to the barn area. The driver turned it around, then backed up to the barn.

"OSU. Great place to go to school, but I'd not live there if they paid me. I don't like city much. I do go over to the Zoo and assist sometimes. Specialty for that is birds. My secondary specialty is avian."

"Did you see her canaries?"

"Every blessed one of them – they're amazing. Remind me to take you up there when we're done here. It's going to be a long day, I'm thinking. Help me line up the crush."

Toby, having worked on some farms in his summers as a teen, knew the crush was a narrow cage that one animal would fit into so it could be attended to with less danger of it getting away or anyone getting hurt.

Dana met them with her mother, both in work gear, wearing leather gloves, carrying leads. "I thought we'd unload our horses first? Sara's sort of skittish and Rebel's not good on ramps."

"Breed?" asked Amanda.

"Both are Tennessee walkers. Mom and I like to ride." She went up into the truck and walked down a beautiful, well-tended animal, who was snorting a little, shaking his head – his version of complaining. He balked at the top of the ramp and had to be coaxed down.

"We won't need the crush for them but Big Al we will."

"Big Al?" asked Alan.

"He's not all that big but thinks he is. He's the bull."

Amanda handed Toby her clipboard with some instructions on what he was to write down on each animal. She carefully went over the horse, checking its legs, looking in its mouth, rewarding it with a small carrot. "He's gorgeous. I have a Morgan but I hear Walkers are great rides."

"They ride like silk feels, is how my mom puts it. Both are taught to neck rein and they handle nicely. I had the men go over some of the old trails and I walked them yesterday to be sure there's no holes or roots so we can do some trail rides."

"Sounds good to me," replied the vet. "Where do we take him?"

"I have outdoor pens set up for everyone, some temp, some permanent. Our horses, Mom and I can lead to the temporary corral. We already have hay and water set up so they can just settle. Bill, can you lead Sara down and we'll get them both done and move on to the cattle."

The horses were done quickly and led away. Bill, the trucker, suggested they open the crush and stand on each side ready to clang it shut. Big Al was not in a good mood. He hated trucks. He hated ramps. He hated being away from his comfortable barn. He was full of attitude and was not going to like whatever was about to happen. He tossed his head and snorted.

Big Al was a miniature Highland bull, about forty inches tall, around six hundred pounds, but obviously not realizing he wasn't as big as a standard bull. He grunted as a lead was clipped to him and with a little bit of help in the form of a handful of carrot chips, trotted down the ramp and into the crush.

Toby laughed.

"What's the matter?" asked Dana.

"Well, my friend Sammy's dad raises longhorns. When you said Big Al, I had visions of, well, nothing like this. He's sort of cute in a mad, shaggy kinda way."

The vet grinned. "Yeah. I've seen the longhorns."

Dana said, "Highlands have a downy undercoat I brush out in the late spring and it spins beautifully. He's a crazy animal, but he's never tried to chase us or anything. He has his own little corral waiting. He gets along well with the horses." They completed his check-up, and he was led off by Dana to his small corral next to the horses. His five females were examined and placed on the other side of the horses. The cattle were followed by baby doll southdown sheep, seven ewes and one male, each around two foot tall.

Two tall llama geldings came out, heads nearly at seven feet, strolling in an imperial way, owning whatever they laid their eyes on. They were followed by one male alpaca who was placed with the bull, and ten female alpaca – six white, one light grey, one rose grey, one fawn colored, one black. A large dog, which they were told was an Anatolian Shepherd, followed them. He got his yearly booster shot and made friends with the vet easily after he was convinced he couldn't sit on her feet. Several carrier pens of rabbits were carried out and into the barn where their roomy new pens waited them. Five pyagora goats came out next, all ewes, all pregnant. Lastly, a carrier with three long haired cats were carried to the house. Two barn cats were added to the barn.

"The house cats are a Persian and two Himalayan. I raise them downstairs. They don't go up with the birds, ever. I already have Cantor inside and you can look at him when we step in to see the house animals." Dana watched the animals as they settled in to their paddocks.

"Cantor?" Amanda asked.

"He's a Maine coon and he sings a lot." The vet nodded as if that made perfect sense.

Mrs. McCallister spoke up. "Don't forget Giz."

"Giz?" asked Alan.

"He's an Amazon parrot. He talks and I use his shed feathers to make jewelry."

Alan shook his head. "You ought to charge admission. A few more animals and you'd have a zoo."

Dana laughed. "Yeah, been told that before. I used to hold yarn retreats out until too many people had allergies to cats or dogs or birds and it got all complicated. I may want to talk to your mom about that."

"You know mom?" he asked as he held cats for the vet to check over.

"I knew you had to be the boy she talks so much about as soon as you drove up. She told me about the truck. I had one like it when I was in college, lo, those many moons ago," she smiled at him and then continued. "Anyway, the barn cats are needed for vermin control out here. And now, that's everyone, let me pay Bill so he can leave."

"Got one more," he replied.

"What? That's all we had at the farm."

"Your friend back home said you'd wanted one and since she had one, we loaded it up and I fetched it to you." He walked up and reached over a divider wall, coming up with a grunt and carrying out the smallest burro the vet had ever seen. "She said his mom had died of milk fever and you need to bottle feed him."

"Oh, for goodness sake! Look at those eyes!" exclaimed Mrs. McCallister, Dana's mom, hurrying over. "Give me that baby. Did she send us proper milk for a burro?"

"She's pretty heavy, why don't you let Alan here carry her for you? And your friend sent a note and this bag of milk replacer. Here's my invoice. We're officially empty and I need to make it to a farm over to Millersburg to take a load back."

"Thank you so much, give me a sec." Dana pulled out a checkbook from a back pocket, wrote out the check, and handed it to the trucker. "Thanks for being so patient, Bill."

"Just got a long drive next back home, no reason to rush it," he answered. "You need anything hauled; you call."

"I will," she smiled as he got into the truck, started it up and drove down the drive, then turned to Alan and Dr. Zoland. "And let me pay you guys, but oh, just feel how soft this little fella is. Doctor Zoland, what can we do to insure he lives? Losing his mom like that and then a long truck drive doesn't make for a happy baby."

"Looks like they have the right feed," she replied, checking the bag. "I'm going to give him a booster shot of things to raise his immune system. The thing to worry about is the scours, of course. Where are you keeping him?"

Dana looked at the house and nodded as she decided, "I'm keeping him on the back porch. It's easy to clean and enclosed and we'll just make a good layer of bedding in one corner. But first, let me get a bottle of milk down him."

Bill had handed the baby off to Alan, who carried it to the house for Dana and her mom. Dana ran to the barn and brought back a bale of straw, which she broke open and covered one end of the porch with, moving a rocker out of the way and a small wicker table. Her mother came up with a sheep panel that fit nicely across the end of the porch, making a six-by-six enclosure. Alan simply cuddled the baby as the vet gave it a shot, took its temperature, and calmed it down.

Dana went into the house, prepared a bottle, and came back. She got into the pen and sat down, and Alan handed her the burro who started to chug the bottle immediately. Mrs. McCallister took out her camera and snapped shots of the new baby. He finished quickly and Dana snuggled him down into the straw and left the pen to take the vet in to see the indoor pets. They could hear the canaries singing overhead.

"I can't spin his fleece but they make good deterrents to dogs, even the miniatures. I'll probably keep him with the goats. At any rate, he's so darling. Now, did you think the stock was ok? Do I need to keep an eye out for anything?"

"I think you take great care of your animals," Amanda as she took the cats out of their carriers one by one and did a check on them. They were glad to be free and purred loudly. Another cat wandered in from the back room, sounding a little like a small chain saw. He stopped in mid buzz and growled/talked and complained as he rubbed up against his owner. "If you have any problems call me."

Alan grinned and got down to pet the cat. The cat accepted the petting as his just due. "This has to be Cantor," he said.

"That's him. He's really gentle but he yowls a lot. And that Persian is St. Ives, the other two are Alistair and Cleopatra." She paused. "Alan, you ever work in your mom or dad's shops?"

"Yes, but I'm not working in the shop this year. You know, Dad said they'd had several ladies come in to see the drop spindles, and folks are signing up for the class, and Mom asked you to consider adding another class because you may have an overage. And she said those drop spindle kits are selling out and wondered if you had any more set up?"

"I shall definitely set up a second class as soon as this all settles and I do have more kits and I'll take them with me when I go into town."

"Then we're going to be seeing each other a bit," said Dr. Zoland. "I just signed up for that class." She wrote out an invoice and gave it to Dana.

"It will be a pleasure having you." She handed a check to the vet, who entered it into her laptop. Dana and Mrs. McCallister went back to settle the animals as the vet team went to their trucks.

Once back at the clinic, Amanda explained the process for the afternoon to Alan. He spent the afternoon assisting with dogs and cats and one python.

At five, he checked out and headed for home. *I think this summer is going to be an absolute blast. I'm going to show the pics I took to Mom; she's going to want to come out and see that donkey for sure,* he said to himself as he left.

Chapter Six

Brad added the evidence bag with the drop spindle to the file. He studied the thing; it was obviously 3-D printed, brightly colored lime green with a hot pink whorl. Not the sort of thing Amish would have. Jammed through the screen on the door hardly seemed like the sort of thing Amish would do themselves, either, and what did this have to do with the fire?

Jed came into his office. "Hey, got a weird." he remarked, sitting down.

"I do weird occasionally."

"You got any idea what this is?" he handed Brad another drop spindle, this one wooden, made of some sort of hard wood that had been polished.

"Where'd you get it?"

"Boy at the schoolyard had it chasing kids with it, trying to poke them. Teacher confiscated it, and since I was in the neighborhood, had me talk to the monkey about running and chasing people with sharp objects. Wife has one sort of like it from the fiber shop; doing a class or some such thing."

"What kid?"

"Preacher's oldest boy, what's his name," he started looking through his paperwork.

"David. It figures. Did he say where he'd got it?"

"He got kind of weaselly about that. Said an old lady had given it to him."

"Yeah. Seem to be a lot of old ladies lately. Well, I'll see him at lunch. And I have another one left at the barn burning. I think they go together but not sure how. You get your report to me when it's done and I'll add it to the file."

Brad looked at his watch, thought a moment, and decided to head out for the school. He made a short stop at the Fiber Mavens. "Hi, ladies," he said cheerfully. "You aren't missing anything, are you?"

"Don't think so," replied Lydia. "What might we be missing?" Allyssa came over as well, and Clarissa stayed at the register with her ears up. Her nose always twitched when she was trying to listen in. Thom called it her gossip's nose.

Brad held up the evidence bags with spindles. Allyssa took them and studied them. "Those could have come from here. Our new teacher Dana put out twenty assorted drop spindles and ten kits. The kits are sold but there are a few spindles left. Let's check." She walked over to the spinning corner and examined the spindle display. "Some are wood, some are plastic, different styles, but this one is yellow and is made like your green one and this little one here is made like your wooden one, but I think it's cherry. Yours looks like pine."

Brad nodded. "So, they could have come from here?"

"They've been selling fast. I sent word to her to bring in more."

"Ok, so do you keep a list of who buys them?"

"Only a list of the ones signing up for classes, I'm afraid. The rest we just check out."

He nodded. "Well, at least I've got a possible point of purchase. Anyone odd signing up for classes?"

"No," replied Allyssa as she went over to the sign-up sheet and read it. "Most the Fiber Mavens have already signed up and we're going to hold two groups now, talked it over with Dana last night. Plus Casey and Annie, and myself and Suzanne and Aurora and my goodness, we have 25 signed up. Might need three classes. I think I can safely give you a copy of these lists if you want; they're not really confidential hanging up on the board. And you know pretty much everyone on them."

"Well, sort of keep an eye out, will you? I might eventually need to a copy of the sign-up sheet, but I know all these people and don't think any of them would do anything other than spin with these."

"Has something happened?"

"I'm not even sure of that yet. Thank you kindly for your help."

Chapter Seven

Allyssa settled the ladies into their seats. She welcomed each one by name as they sat down and then Allyssa stood up in front of them.

"Welcome to the next new thing here at Fiber Mavens. I'd like to welcome our newest fiber artist, Dana McCallister, who comes to us from Indiana by way of, I think, Pennsylvania, Texas, Alaska, South America, Switzerland, Vermont, and Wisconsin."

"My heavens!" exclaimed Mazie Bradler. She owned Blue Dawn Fibers. "I thought I'd made it to a lot of fiber shows, but I've never left the states."

Allyssa smiled. "According to this biography, she was married to a military man and she traveled all over the world with him. He and her son are recently passed." The entire group of ladies lowered their eyes and sighed. "However, ever since she was a child, she has been a fiber artist, as her mother Ethel McCallister was a fiber artist before her and still is. Dana has a degree in Fine Arts from Cornell University in New York, and she has been a fiber judge for the past five years. She raises her own animals to spin from, but has friends all around the world who exchange fibers from her farm to theirs. I met her last year at the Fiber and Arts show in Ashland; she was judging the fleece competition and had a booth where she was selling rovings – such wonderful rovings! When I found out she was moving here, I asked if she'd like to help teach people here and she said she'd love it. She's in the process of completing her move and according to my secret tall, dark, son source, she has a baby burro out at her farm, among other things. At any rate, I'm taking this class too because I'm curious as the rest of you on how to make my own yarn. Let's welcome Dana to the Fiber Mavens!"

The ladies applauded and Dana stood up. "Thank you so much. If you would not mind, could you each introduce yourself, just go around the circle, so I can put faces with this attendance sheet? I like to know folks."

"Let me start. I'm Allyssa Martin and I own the shop and have the cutest, smartest son in the entire world." The ladies tittered among themselves, then the next spoke up.

"And he's going to be a great vet! My name is Amanda Zoland, I'm new in town, and I'm the vet he's learning from this summer. You're right to be proud of him. You raised him right and he's a good kid." Allyssa looked delighted as she beamed back at Amanda.

"My names is Casey Malcom and this is my daughter Annie. The angels who right now are asleep here in this carrier are Kai and Enya and my mom would be watching them but she's here too,"

"And they're darling," replied Dana. "Your husband is the detective?"

"That's him."

"Good, having the police around makes us all feel safer. And where is your mom?"

"Here I am, my name Sandra Armstrong," she waved from her seat next to some older ladies and they went back to comparing their spindles and roving.

Dana smiled and turned back to the next person. "And you are?"

"My name is Betsy Bayou and my husband Jed is the deputy. I work at the school as a receptionist."

"I'm Sophia Drummel and I am not too old to learn something new. My best friend knew how to do this and so did my ma and I want to keep up with my ancestors. Besides, I could make Pierre a jacket made from yarn I spun myself."

"That's a good goal. I take it that's Pierre under your chair?" She gestured at the sleeping tiny dog.

"He's waiting for his tea. He particularly likes chamomile."

"I see. And you are?" Dana asked another woman.

"I'm Rosemary Collins. I think I may be older than Sophia and I think neither of us are too old to learn something new. Although somehow, I have already mislaid my spindle and can't find it. I tried to get here early to buy another one before class."

"I agree with that sentiment," smiled Dana. "And no worries, use one of mine and after class go choose another one." She handed Rosemary a pretty walnut drop spindle.

"I'm Aurora Anderson. I teach fifth grade at the school."

"I am Mayellen Yoder and I am here with my friend Hannah Byler. She's a baker. I am a farmer's wife."

"And Mayellen makes incredible blankets for preemie babies and hats for the cancer patients," added Allyssa. "And Hannah brought the cookies tonight."

"She did? Awesome," enthused the next person. "My name is Melody Bibby and I run the bookstore."

She nodded to the next person in the circle who said, "I'm Jane Long and my niece here is Andy; our family has the Get A Long Cafe." Dana nodded.

"And I'm Suzanne Hays and I own the sister store here, Fabric Avalanche. I love learning new things."

"Thank you. So altogether, fifteen of us. All the time my husband was in the military, all I could think about was getting my own place and settling down with my family and animals. You really get so tired of being deployed here, there, and everywhere. He was a specialist in what he did and so we moved fairly often to new installations. For instance, my son was born in Texas and in three weeks, we moved to Germany for six months and then to Hawaii and back to Texas. We did that for over fifteen years. That's all over now, and Mom and I are having a good time setting up our farm. In a few weeks, I want to take you all out there for a tour and tea, but for now, let's get started with tonight's project.

"Now do you all have one of the kits or at least a spindle? Excellent. Let me give you a little background on drop spindles. The earliest drop spindles we have date from almost 7000 years ago and were found in tombs in the Middle east. Actually, they only found the whorls, that's this bottom part because the wooden part, the shaft, had rotted away. Whorls of different kinds have been found in almost every area on the globe made of stones, wood, semiprecious stones, horn, and everything in between. The earliest fibers were spun simply by rolling them on your leg, then they added a stick to catch what you had rolled and someone added a weight and here we have drop spindles. Drop spindles were used all the way up to the 16th century when spinning wheels took over. A drop spindle has three parts, the shaft, which is the stick part, the whorl, which is the weight at the top or bottom of the shaft and a hook. I see most of you have top spinners, I use both top and bottom spindle dependent on my fiber. In the middle ages and before, everyone spun fiber – men, wives, kids – because it takes so long to get enough to make fabric. Fabric was very precious. So they would spin at night by the fire, they would spin as they walked from place to place, they would spin as they watched over flocks in the fields. In medieval times, part of a family's taxes would be a pound of yarn spun up; some places even asked men to work on the roads three days a year and the wives and daughters to come to the palace three days out of a year and spin for them. Usually, a family would spin their yarns for different purposes, depending on what fleece they had, heavy wools for cloaks and blankets, lighter for close to the skin fabrics. They would prepare it, dye it and then take it to a weaver for being made into cloth."

She paused and pulled some roving and some yarn out of her bag. "Let's get a feel for what we have in our hands first by tying a leader yarn here on your spindle," she handed out eighteen inches of yarn to each person and helped them tie them in the correct place. "I have a handout for you about spindles and it goes back over the history in greater detail and all my instructions so don't worry about making notes. You won't need them. You will need your hands free for tonight." She continued her class, correcting errors and shortly most of the ladies had successfully managed to make a few feet of yarn. They softly chattered as they worked, each helping the other, making the room feel companionable with no one seeming left out.

"Now, let's take a short break and then come back to practice some more. Once you are confident you can produce a uniform piece of ply, we'll look at this week's homework."

The ladies all got up and got cookies and tea or coffee, came back, and settled in for a bit of gossiping, which is what made classes so much fun. Sophia took a little bowl out of her pocket, put some cream in it, half filled it with tea and sat it down for Pierre, who actually did lick it up, genteelly burping afterwards, requesting with big eyes at his mistress to be let out to go potty and, when he came back in, finally trotting over to Sophia's chair and sitting under it again. She gave him a chew toy and he settled in. Dana got better acquainted with everyone. She had agreed to start another class the next week on Tuesday. They split the 27 who had signed up into two groups, one meeting tonight with 15 and the other next Tuesday with, at this point, twelve.

After thirty minute or so, Dana called them all back to work and they practiced for a while. The quietly continued their discussions started at the break. Dana let them work for another forty minutes, then handed out her lessons and said, "Now I am going to give each of you a small bag of roving. This is a blend of merino and llama, long fibers so it ought to be easy for you to practice with. I'd like you all to have it spun up into single ply yarn by next week, but I also want you to have it split into two mostly the same size balls of first step yarn. Make it as thin as you like, remembering it is going to added to another piece to make two ply yarn. I personally like mine to be about like this," and she passed around a couple pieces for them to look at. "Next week we are going to learn to ply. What I am handing out are the natural colors of my animals, it's not dyed, so you may have either grey, brown, cream or black. There's about two ounces to practice with. Next week we will ply it, set it, and hang it to dry. You will learn about how to figure out what weight of whorl you need for what fiber, and you'll be given a pattern to take home to use with your yarn when it's dry. Once dried, we'll be making it into a simple knitted or crocheted scarf so you'll be able to say you made this scarf from beginning to end. See you all next week!"

Chapter Eight

Brad walked over to the school where he had visited at lunch time every day for the past five years. He took his sack lunch out of his bag, along with another bag of cookies, and went to sit down on "his" bench, near the playground. He poured himself a cup of coffee from his thermos and took out his sandwich. He sometimes missed getting food from the cafe, but he had to admit the sandwiches his wife made were lots better. Today's seemed to be a combination of turkey, cheese, lettuce, bacon, tomato, pickles, sweet onions, some sort of sauce, all on a hoagie bun with sesame seeds on top. She'd included a little bag of chips, and a note reminding him of the class she would be at tonight, where to find his supper, and how much she loved him. He smiled and tucked it into his pocket, took a bite of his sandwich and looked up. He thought he saw something over by the sidewalk, a glimpse of red and blue. He followed it up the trunk of a large tree and amidst the starting to turn fall colors, he saw movement. On the sidewalk, someone walked by, ducked and hurried on, brushing their heads. There was a definite sound of giggling. He watched a moment longer, sighed, put his sandwich back in its bag and walked over.

"Ok, get down here." he demanded.

The tree was quiet.

"I mean now. I can see you. Get down here." A glob of something white and icky looking hit the pavement next to him.

"Assaulting an officer with goop is punishable offense. You want me to cuff you two?"

The tree shook a little as two boys, the older one carrying a quart jar, came slowly down.

David and Bryan wore wearing guilty expressions.

Brad took the jar and stirred it. "What is this stuff?"

"It's fake bird poop," exclaimed Bryan proudly. "We made it in science class."

"David?"

"It's a non-Newtonian fluid. That means it doesn't follow Newton's law, like ketchup, you know, you shake it and it gets thinner so you can pour it? Honey and peanut butter are too, and they're inventing a liquid bullet proof vest. We did make it in science lab. We were mixing it and stuff, it's mostly cornstarch and glue and stuff, and Jimmy picked some up and dropped it and it hit with a splat and he said it was like pigeon poop and, I don't know, it just sort of snowballed from there."

"David swiped the jar before recess and we came out here and have been dropping it on people and it's been funny," grinned his little brother. "It won't stain or anything. And no one gets hurt. It just goes plop on your head or whatever." Seeing the officers face he shut up and stopped smiling. "Are we in trouble?"

"Let's see, you stole from the classroom, you're out way past recess, so technically you're truant, you've been attacking people with a science experiment, so that's assault, and you've made me miss my lunch. Would you think you were in trouble?"

Just then, Aurora Anderson and Miss Beckley came across the park. "And here come your teachers, right on time, and I think you've got trouble. And if they don't give you enough hell," the little boys eyes got big at his use of a bad word, "then when I talk to your dad, I suspect you're going to have even bigger trouble."

"Good afternoon, ladies," he said politely. "Would you be looking for the boys?"

"We would indeed and I see you've got our experiment which is supposed to be sitting on the table settling for the next class," said Mrs. Anderson. "Just how did that get out here?"

The sheriff gave the teachers a rundown of the last hours activities. Their faces passed through the unlikely progression of relief, disbelief, upset, and into two women desperately trying not to laugh at the latest antic of the pastor's boys.

"I think I see some detentions coming on," said Ms. Beckley. "Thank you kindly for capturing them, but if you can put them back into our custody, we'll handle this as an internal affair."

"Strikes me that some external application might be in order, but we can have their dad do that. Shall I cuff them for you?"

"Oh, I don't think that's necessary," smiled Aurora. "Missing recess for a week, and afterschool chores for the week as well, ought to make them think a bit about their sins."

"I'm rather fond of writing out the seventh commandment five hundred times, but this is a public school," replied Brad. "However, I can get the secular for you from the Revised Code. It's nearly thirty pages long, the section on stealing and the various types. Handwriting thirty pages a few times might take them until Christmas but could make them into lawyers." The boy's faces were approaching abject horror as each punishment was discussed, each one worse than the last.

"I'd consider that a fate worse than death," answered Ms. Beckley. "The lawyering, not the writing. The writing could teach them exactness and to be more careful. If you could just sort of email that text to me as an attachment?"

"No!" gasped David. "Softball season just started last week. I have after school practice. I can't spend the time writing. I have to learn to pitch."

"Pitching may take a back burner to whatever the officer has to say," came a voice. They all turned to see Pastor Atherton standing quietly with his arms folded. "Just what have you two been doing this time?"

The pastor checked out the really quite interesting glop in the jar, the boy's faces and abject demeanor, heard the story and said," How many people did you actually hit with this stuff?"

"I don't know."

"I think you do."

"There was old Mrs. Drummond, and she said a bad word, and a couple Amishmen, who said something in German, and a couple high schoolers and the detective and that old lady whose spinner we found," he stuttered.

"Back up, what old lady?"

"The one that gave David the spinner."

"Did she actually give it to you?"

"No, she just dropped it and kept walking and I picked it up and studied it and then Bill called me and I ran over to the class but the teacher caught me with it and then the detective came."

"I see. Anyone else?"

"No, the rest we sort of missed."

"There's a lot of non-Newtonian fluid missing and we needed the entire bottle for class," replied his teacher. "You will need to stand before the class when we go back and apologize for ruining science class for today. You will miss the points from the afternoon lab quiz and everyone else will get full points. You will stay in for the week after school for thirty minutes cleaning the room, and you will write an essay overseen by your father, no less than three hundred words, on the evils of stealing, due Friday. Do you understand?"

David nodded glumly. His little brother looked up hopefully at his second-grade teacher.

"Bryan, I know you just followed your big brother, but you could have turned back at any time. You will miss all recesses this week. You will write fifty times, 'I will not steal again.' Your father can do at home whatever he feels is right about this, but until this is completed before Friday, you will consider yourself on room arrest: no recess, no prizes, and you need to sit in the back thinking-chair corner for the rest of the week by yourself to do your work. Do you understand?"

"Yes, ma'am." He was biting his lower lip to avoid crying.

"Pastor Atherton, David will be home late tonight."

"I will be waiting when he comes home."

"You boys run back to the classroom. I shall call the aide and tell her what is to be done now," said Ms. Anderson, pulling out her cell. "March right now."

The boys ran/walked across the park. When they were over half way across, Brad started to chuckle, the teachers joined him, and soon all four adults had given into their impulse to laugh.

Sheriff Black came upon them as they were starting to settle down. "I don't see a flock of pigeons," he said. "I've been getting complaints, and so has the mayor that the pigeons are overrunning the park. Lots of droppings," he was interrupted by the laughter starting up again. The two teachers shook their heads and turned back to the school. The pastor wiped his eyes.

Brad was left to explain to the sheriff who, halfway through, started chuckling and got out his phone. "I'll just call over to the Mayor's office and let him know we stopped the bombing and dispersed the pigeons. Sheesh! Those boys remind me of me when I was that age." He shook his head. "I came over to let you know there's been another spindle issue."

"Oh?"

"Appears that six or seven of them have come up missing at the fiber shop. Allyssa is really upset and says she doesn't think any of her ladies would have done that. They were in some sort of bucket or jar or something. Anyway, Jed took the report but thought you'd want to add it to the other two cases."

"Well, one of them is solved. One of those spindles belongs to an older lady and David had it. She dropped it and rather than give it back, he chased other kids with it. Kid has more energy than sense."

Just then, there was the sound of running feet. The two boys in question had run back from the school.

"Officer Brad?" asked David. "We have to go back to school but mom always told us if we hurt somebodies' feelings or anything, we ought to apologize. I haven't figured out how we're going to apologize to the other people, but we're going to apologize to the class at school and we want to say we're sorry for causing you trouble and making you miss your lunch."

"Thank you. I appreciate that. And I want to ask you to do something for me."

"What's that?"

"Come over to the car." He led them over, got into the trunk and pulled out a small book.

"A bunch of kids work with me helping keep our town safe. I want you to consider joining our group of detectives. Before you earn your badges, you have to read this book, cover to cover and tell me what you think of becoming one of my Irregulars." He handed them a book for kids of Sherlock Holmes Mysteries that happened to focus on Sherlock as a child. He'd gotten a couple dozen copies and thus far had made good use of them among the younger set at the school.

"What?" asked David. "You want us to be deputies?"

"Read the book and then read it to your brother, and we'll talk. And don't get into any more trouble. Now scoot."

He stood up and shut the trunk lid.

"That a good idea?"

"I've found if you give kids a nudge in the right direction, they can be really helpful. And it will keep them out of trouble. I hope. I'll run over and see the Fiber Mavens."

Chapter Nine

"Here we are, Mom," announced Casey as her mother opened the door. "Kai gets pretty excited when he knows we're pulling up to your house. Enya is just quiet and watches everything with those big blue eyes."

"Well, of course. This is the official spoil-a-grandchild center," she grinned. "Kai, you just wait to see what we're going to get into today! Enya, I have a new teddy bear for you."

Casey laughed. "I'll be back by lunch. I just have morning visits and then back home."

"I thought that man of yours had you convinced to stay home?"

"He tried. But Mom, there are so many hurting people out there. As long as this little man can have good care from his dad or his sister or grandma, I can do at least a little to alleviate the pain."

Knowing her daughter and that further argument would not end well, Mrs. Armstrong changed the subject. "What did you think of the new spinning teacher?"

"She was lovely. I can't wait to take ourselves out to meet her flocks. Brad promised to get me a bar stool to sit on so I have a farther drop for the spindle."

"A bar stool! That's a good idea. Tell him to snag one for me."

"He said he'll ask Finian. I'll tell him at least three, for Annie wants one, too." The Finian in question ran Finian's Fine Furniture Store, a place that dealt in new and old furniture, an eclectic group of both. You might find a modern couch sitting next to 1950's kitchen dinettes, or a Queen Anne chair next to end tables made of logs. It sounds jarring, but somehow, Finian made it all work well. The idea he could have some errant bar stools somewhere in the warehouse didn't surprise anyone. In fact, he had recently pulled several spinning wheels of various vintage out to display, as so many people were talking about them right now. He'd asked Dana to come in and make sure they had all their pieces. Three of the five were in perfect shape, and she bought two of them on the spot; the others she explained where to get parts to repair them, so he figured to sell them soon. She'd told him the ones she bought weren't antiques, they were simply Ashford travelers, but she needed them for the classes and he'd given her a good price for them. The remaining working wheel was a Kromski.

Anyway, he'd told Brad he had some bar stools, could not guarantee they matched each other but they were sturdy and serviceable. Brad had told Casey he'd get them for her this afternoon. Casey explained this to her mother.

"Well, that's good," said her mother. "We'll have them in time to help with the homework. How are you doing? Which roving did you get?"

"I chose cream because I want to try dying it. Annie took copper colored."

"I got black. It will go well with my coat. I can't get over how soft this stuff feels."

"It does. Allyssa told me they'd shortly be handling some other rovings in dyed colors in the shop. I can't wait to see them. Well, I need to be off. One more kiss, there, on my way to my client."

"You be careful."

"I always am."

Casey drove off, considering how nice early fall weather felt. Leaves against the blue sky were gorgeous, yellows, reds, oranges, and some sort of a lime green – they'd softened from their dark green and, against the other leaves, stood out like beacons. The assorted white and Scotch pines here and there gave the small hills outside the feel of a warm patchwork quilt, covering the hills, putting them all to sleep for winter. Here and there farmers were out finishing the hay harvest, or soybeans or planting winter wheat. Some of the Amish fields had actual corn shucks standing up in them, like tilted old giants, stooping in the fields in neat rows. She followed progressively smaller roads until she reached gravel roads and then a long lane, where she pulled in. Her client lived back here on a secluded farm.

Casey left her windows down; there wasn't a sign of rain. She left her briefcase and took her bag to the door, where she was met by a tired farm mother with three kids. The children were set aside to work on a game and the mother sat down to talk about the week with Casey. Sometimes Casey thought that just having a listening ear was all the folks needed, just someone to listen and trust. They were willing to make changes if they could just see why. Casey's job as a therapist was to aid them in finding ways to make changes that would make their lives and their families lives more stable. She interjected some ideas and options here and there, but for most of the back-country clients, she would be the only other person besides their family that they would see, sometimes for weeks at a time. The session hour seemed to pass quickly. Casey gave each of the children a sticker for being quiet, and left.

When she got back to her car she groaned. Sitting in her back seat, acting as if he owned it, sat a goat. She was pretty sure it had just come through the window but her lunch bag was rapidly being chewed up and swallowed. She went back to the house and knocked on the door.

"Excuse me, Mrs. Roberts. I seem to have gotten inhabited while we were in. You think your boy could come out and take the goat out of the car?"

"Oh, heaven's sake, I hope he hasn't caused any damage." The mother and her kids came out and hauled the goat out of the car. "I can't imagine why she'd do that!" Poor Mrs. Roberts was so embarrassed.

"I suspect it was the sandwich in my lunch bag. It ought not harm her and I'm not really hungry, and doesn't appear he got into anything else. Is she expecting?"

"All the goats are bred right now."

"She was just nibbly, that's all. No real harm done." Casey reached in and brushed the seat off, then noticed the spindle on the floor.

"Now that's odd. Do you spin? Pretty sure the goat doesn't."

"No, lands, I'd not have time for such doings. Pretty thing though."

"I can't imagine how it got in the back seat. My spindle is at home."

"Can I make you a sandwich?" asked Mrs. Roberts.

"Oh, no, I'm fine. I have to get along. I have three more calls to make today. You remember to do your calming exercises, morning and evening."

Casey drove off. The car smelled vaguely of goat so she left the windows down. She got back to the main road and saw her husband driving by, so she honked the horn. He waved and kept going. He had Jed with him so they were most likely off on a case. She waited for traffic and looked at the spindle. It was solid wood, the whorl being some dark shade she guessed was walnut. It was indeed a pretty thing. "I'll have a story to tell Brad this evening," she thought to herself. "Goats in the car leaving spindles. At least someone is giving out good stuff and causing no harm this time. Two more clients and a quick stop to enter the data in the computer and I'll pick up the babies."

Chapter Ten

"It's a good crowd," remarked Brad as he and Jed pulled up to the Hershberger's farm.

"Great day for a barn raising," he replied. "They were able to save some of it. What happened to the boys on Rumspringer?"

"Rumspringa, and they're in their parents' custody. There's some doubt in my mind as to motive here. I talked it over with the sheriff and judge and we've got a plan. I'm here to talk to the boys and their father's at intermission, so to speak. Here they come now."

The three Amish fathers were headed his way, followed by three boys whose heads were bowed down a bit as they followed.

"Brad, why are you doing this in public? Normally you would meet in private?" Jed was concerned.

"The boys' dads wanted it public. They apologize in public for their sins and it's my understanding the boys apologized in church last week, so everyone will know why we're here. And yeah, I'm not comfortable, but it's a culture thing." They men got out of the car and headed towards the Amishmen, stopping after ten feet as they came to meet the officers.

"Morning, Jacob, Enoch, David," nodded Brad. "Great day for a barn raising."

"Yah, we come together always to help each other," replied David, extending his hand to shake. "The burnt parts were cleaned out last week by family mostly, and our barn expert came and let us know what was needed, so we had the wood all here and in place and now it's getting done. While we're at it, we're enlarging a little, adding to one end. It will be good when it's done. But admiring our new barn isn't why you've come?"

"No, it's not. However, can the young men involved come up here where I can see them?" The boys, who had been partially hidden behind their fathers, now reluctantly stepped around them and stood closer to the officers.

"Boys, there is some doubt in our minds as to how much of this was deliberate, and how much was foolish error. For sure, hiding fireworks in a barn wasn't the smartest thing to do, but, thank goodness, you'd not hidden them in your bedroom or basements. Taking them from an older person you didn't know was maybe not so wise either, and we've yet to find the old lady who allegedly gave them to you. Firing them off behind the firehouse was most likely in the category of being foolish, not being spiteful. After discussion with the sheriff and the local juvenile court judge, they're content with this, and we'll see what your folks have to say about it as well.

"For the firehouse incident, you are ordered to take a fire safety course at the firehouse and to put in ten hours of community service for them. That means for two days this month – and your folks may choose which days – you come to the firehouse, take a safety course, and do ten hours of cleaning or gardening. That's for one infraction. For the infraction of possession of illegal fireworks, you are put on non-reporting probation for six months and assigned another ten hours of community service to be performed in your local community; this is not doing chores at home. You need to help someone else for ten hours, perhaps an older person needs wood chopped for winter or their yard mowed, that sort of thing. They can't be related to you and maybe your pastor or bishop would have ideas on that one."

Unbeknown to the boys, their bishop had come up and was listening. He'd been assisting at the barn raising and quietly spoke, nodding at the officers as he came. "I have some ideas, for certain. Boys, you know Widow Yoder, lives over on Boxman road? Her house needs scraped and painted; her chicken house needs repair. We will provide the paint and tools; you shall provide the labor and I will provide the supervision. It may take more than ten hours."

"That brings me to the last charge, setting the barn on fire. The judge thought helping with the rebuilding on the day it was rebuilt was a good start, but he also thought another ten hours of community service wouldn't hurt. So, on the three charges, you have thirty house of community service, ten to be in town because one of the acts was in town, the others out here with your own people who are the ones who suffered the most from your shenanigans. Now, frankly, the judge could have ordered you into juvenile jail for six months on just one of these so I think he's being lenient on you. You are not to get into any more such silliness. I mean, yes, you are on rumspringa, but there are limits to that. Have fun, but within the law and with common sense. You want to buy some jeans and a cell phone and try out movies or go to parties, fine. Don't hurt anyone. Oh, and except for the community service in town, you have to be on your parent's farm or at church or in the presence and control of your mom or dad for the next thirty days. We call it grounding. I have it all written out here and copies for each of you, and I made a copy for the bishop as well." He handed papers to each person who needed one.

The bishop nodded. "It seems fair and just. We will all comply. When they have completed their service, what then?"

"Just let me know and I'll have it stamped completed. A written statement from you, signed by the boys as well, acknowledging their work, would be good for us to have in their files when it's all done."

"I shall do that. Thank you. Would you like to join us at meal? The ladies have cooked up some fine food."

"I have no doubt, but we have a couple more calls. Thank them all for us." He looked over at the gathering of people and studied a moment. "Isn't that Rosemary Collins over there?"

The bishop looked. "Yes, it is. She married outside the faith and was gone from us for years. She moved back here into town and she comes to see her family. She is a lonely woman and it does her sister good to talk. She brought some food and she helped the women and she is careful not to cross any lines. Since she had not joined the church at the time she left, she was not shunned."

"Interesting. She and Sophia seem to be close."

"Mrs. Drummond? Another good person. Yes, they are close friends. I won't keep you longer. Have a good day, officer." The bishop, carrying his papers, flanked by the fathers and their sons, turned and marched away to eat. Brad and Jed returned to the squad car and drove down the driveway and onto the street.

Brad slowed down to look back at the group. "We could learn a lot from those people," he said quietly. "Unity, cooperation, hard work … good folks."

"You think the boys have learned their lesson?"

"I suspect they will by the time Bishop Yoder is done with them. Those fellows are in for twenty hours at hard labor."

Chapter Eleven

Pastor Atherton leaned back with a relaxed smile on his
face. "It appears you both have a good handle on finances,
you've agreed you want to have kids, you know where you're
going to live, your work schedules are meshed, you have a good
handle on the commitment of marriage, and our final
topic is the outlaws amongst your in-laws." He smiled. "I am
assuming you both know each other's families?"

Toby glanced at Helen. "She knew my mother before Mom
passed, and she's met my brothers' wives and families. I met
her dad and her son. Little Skylar seems to be getting along with
me so far, right, Helen?"

"Sky can't wait for us to be together," she smiled. "I had a
talk with him about maybe us getting a couple other sibs
someday and he wants them to arrive full grown and ready to
play. I sort of disabused him of that idea, but he's ok with Toby.
He said he'd just have to play with Toby until his brothers-to-be
grew up."

Toby chuckled. "He's a great kid. My relatives mostly live
out of state, but Liam and Marti are here local. Helen babysits
for them sometimes."

"We get along fine," she added. "I have a question though.
I'm not a member of a church and Toby here sometimes goes to
the little home church group because it feels more comfortable
to him. I'd kind of like to go to this church but I don't know
how Sky would fit in. We haven't visited any church as a family
yet."

"Having a similar worldview always helps when someone is starting a family, and getting married is starting a new family," replied Pastor Atherton. "Being united on the place of worship is an excellent idea. Have you considered visiting each place?"

"I have a problem trusting going into someone's home. He likes it cause its small and intimate which are the exact reasons I wouldn't," she said softly. "The few times I've gone to someone's house it's been to things like Avon parties where someone wanted me to buy something. The few times I've attended church they seem to do the same thing. I believe in God, but I'm not so sure about his church, or any for that matter."

"It's too bad that's been your experience. May I make this suggestion? Since Toby is already attending the house church, why don't the two of you go together this week, and then next week come here and alternate? You said earlier you were a Catholic at one time."

"I tried that and didn't like it very much," she interjected.

The pastor nodded. "Well, then why not sort of experiment a little, and for certain pray about it together. We talked once before about having worship together, at least a prayer, each day before you separated and ran off to the daily grind. Why not make finding a church family one of the things you ask Him about? Here in our little town, you have only two choices, but there are churches within easy driving distance that might fit you better." He reached into his desk and pulled out a list. "This is a list of all the churches within twenty miles of here; there are fourteen. If you both sit down and discuss what you are looking for in a church, then visit them sort of as if you had a checklist, asking God to lead you, you will find the one that fits."

"Those suggestions are not at all what I expected," said Toby. "Most preachers I know try to get you to come to their congregation and wouldn't dream of suggestions to look around."

"Been my experience that folks who are strong-armed into a church don't stay and aren't happy. I don't think that's how God works, so I don't either. You're definitely welcome here. We are pleased to host your wedding. But finding a home church is a work you need to do. Now back to the in-laws and outlaws. Do either of you have any reservations or worries about either side of relatives.?"

They continued their session, with the pastor jokingly reminding them that in three weeks, they'd be tying a knot. He was confident they knew what they were doing and looked forward to the service. "I always did like weddings. I guess it's the same thing as my brother the judge who gets to preside over adoptions. Making new families is relaxing and a great blessing."

Chapter Twelve

"So how did it go? Did you get the two ounces all spun?" asked Dana as she faced her spinning class.

"I proved you can teach an old dog new tricks," announced Sophia, holding up a full spindle. "Isn't this gorgeous?"

"Well done!" said Dana. "I think you're a natural." She circled the group, seeing what had been accomplished.

"Now, I see you pretty much all made two balls of ply. A single ply can be used but it isn't as strong. Tonight, we're going to work on putting two strands together. You need to start by taking the two balls you have made and sitting them in a quart jar or a yarn bowl. I like using two yarn bowls simply because many of my crafts friends make them out of wood – like this one which was made out of a burl and is so pretty – and others are made of pottery or ceramic – like this one made for me by a friend in Maine – see how she layered the glaze so it looks like sunshine over the ocean?" She held up the two bowls. "At any rate, if you read your handouts, I asked you to bring two jars or large cups; did you all get that far?"

Most of the ladies had, some forgot, so Dana handed around quart jars in pairs. "Now, one ball goes into each jar. Pull out the ends like this. You need a different spindle for this, and I brought some, or you need a spinning wheel, I also brought that. Let me hand out plying spindles, notice the shaft is longer and the whorl is heavier. These ones I am handing around are made by a pair of sisters out of river rocks, they're so smooth, and so cool. You want it heavy enough to pull the threads together, but not stretch them. A spindle weighing around two and a half ounces would be ideal. And I forgot to mention a little trick; if, when you are spinning, you simply leave your yarn on the spindle and fill up several spindles, you can use a small laundry basket as a lazy Kate. See? Just push the yarn up to the end and stick the two ends across the basket and have both ends stuck into either side of the basket corner. You can easily pull the yarn up and off the spindle that way. But back to plying our yarn with our jars …”

She went from person to person, explaining the process, and soon all fifteen of the new spinners were having a good time making their plies into yarn. She then took them to the sink and they soaked their yarns in very hot water in one of their jars. While it was cooling, they went to break and refreshments and settled in for a good gossip.

“Did you hear there’s another crime spree starting?” asked Sophia.

“Should we get involved?” asked her friend, Rosemary.

“I don’t know why we ought to. We have lots of folk in the sheriff’s office now. And besides, nothing very dastardly has happened. Except for the pigeon poo.”

“The what?” asked Annie.

“Poo!” declared Sophia with emphasis. “I heard the pastor’s boys had a bucket of it dropping it on people in the park from a tree. Caught red handed.”

Annie laughed out loud. “I heard about that at school. It wasn’t real poo, it was some stuff they made in the little kids’ science lab, sort of like silly putty, shiny and gloopy and stuff. They were caught and they’ve been grounded and set inside for the past week during recess.”

“The poor pastor’s wife has her hands full with those ones!” declared Melody. “Those rascals remind me of my brother at that age. Anyway, what’s this about a spinning mystery?”

"Well, remember I lost my drop spindle and appears those same boys were chasing kids on the school ground with it. Sheriff said I could come pick it up and I will later this week. But the other one was found near the barn burning and that's the one Sophia must be talking about."

"Near the Hershbergers? But the fire was an accident; just some boys on rumspringa who are making amends right now. Why would there be a spindle?"

"That's what we'd like to know!" declared Sophia. "I feel a new case coming on."

"Did anyone else here lose a spindle?" asked Dana.

"No, but there were 8 stolen last week. We had a count of the ones in the jar and when we went to see how many were left the count was off. I'd counted them before I set them out and entered them in inventory, so I know how many you brought in, and I know how many I sold, but there were several missing. I wanted to talk to you about it. Nothing showed up on our cameras or mirrors, so I don't know. One of those could have been at the fire somehow. I don't think any of our ladies would do that."

"I'll bet it was those boys," said Betsy. "Just the kind of mischief they'd get into."

"I don't think so. I've only seen them in here once or twice last summer with their mom. She normally runs errands while they're in school," replied Allyssa. "Anyway, we made out a report and we're keeping our eyes open. It could have been tourists. We've had a bunch in here lately."

"Maybe, but we'll all keep or eyes open," declared Sophia. "Do you think the fiber is cooked enough?"

"It hasn't got to cook," explained Dana. "It has to soak in hot water until it cools but I think it's been long enough. Now let's get it out of the jars, and I'll explain what to do with it when you get home and hand out the patterns for this week's assignments."

The ladies went to the back counter, found their jars and drained them, then gently squeezed out the water and rolled the fiber up in a paper towel. Dana explained how to weight it for drying, then handed out the next project, and they all left, chattering about the possibility of helping the sheriff again.

Dana assisted Allyssa in the straightening up. As they were hauling the box of empty jars and materials out to the truck,

Annie, who was carrying a box noticed something hanging on the door. "Look at that!" she exclaimed. "Someone brought back one of the lost spindles!"

"What?" asked Allyssa. "No, I don't think so." She studied it and got quiet. "I do think we need to take this over to the sheriff."

"Dad's coming to pick us up. You think he needs it?" asked Annie.

"Need what?" asked Brad. He had come around to locate his stepdaughter. "What do I need? Your mom's changing the little guy. He slept pretty well at the station. Sure will be glad when we get our other car out of the garage." He came over to the door. "A spindle hanging on the door? It must have been put here while you were in class."

"I suspect. That's odd," said Dana. "Let me just cut it off."

"Wait a minute. Let me study that a second." He bent over and looked at it without touching it, then took out an evidence bag. "Yeah, that's a weird all right. "

"What's weird?" asked Dana. She was tired after class and just wanted to go home.

"They tied it to your car using a hangmans' noose."

Chapter Thirteen

Brad sat at the picnic table waiting at lunch time. He was eating his sandwich today, biding his time as first one, then another child came by for a cookie and a chat. Deputy Jed came up and joined him with a sandwich of his own.

"You waiting for someone?" asked Jed as he bit into his hoagie.

"Yep. He meets me here on Wednesdays. It's his probation."

"What?" asked Jed. "We got elementary kids on probation?"

"Not officially."

Just then, David and Bryan ran up to grab a cookie. David sat down. Jed shook his head and then nodded. "I get it."

"Hiya, Officer," David said chomping into the chocolate chip cookie.

"Been good?"

"Yes, sir. Haven't got nothing to report though. Nothing exciting is happening in this town." he complained. "And Dad's keeping me pretty busy. I still got work detail and my charts not half full yet."

"Not surprised. You've done some mischief. And it is busy, but not around your house, I don't think. David, are you in Boy Scouts?"

"I'm in Adventurers. That's like scouts except it's run by the church. Mr. Haustead is the scoutmaster. He's teaching us to march in formation like in the army."

"You know how to tie knots?"

"Oh, yeah! We learned that."

"Can you tie me some knots?" asked Brad pulling a length of rope out of his bag. "All I got with me is clothes line."

"That'll do. Which knot you want?"

"Just show me some general knots."

Jed watched with an odd expression on his face. He chewed his sandwich slowly.

"Well, first you got your basic square knot." David quickly pulled the two ends of the rope together and showed them the result. He untied it and went on. "And then you got two half hitches. I like that one. I use it a lot."

"Ah, huh," said Brad, chewing and watching and trying not to notice as Bryan filched another cookie.

"And then you got a slip knot, that's like this."

Jed, clearing his throat, interrupted. "Mr. Haustead teach you how to do a hangman's noose?"

"I've seen pictures but we didn't have that one. I have a sailor's knot."

"You ever seen parachute cord?" asked Jed.

"Paracord? We used that in Adventurers. It's nice and slippery and it works good for practice. I haven't got any because the scoutmaster took all the knots we did to keep them for parents' night. We're going to have a display."

"You ever do any macrame?"

He looked confused. "What is it?"

"Never mind." Brad shook his head at Jed. "Where were you last night at 8 or so?"

"You mean at night? I'm still grounded, remember. After my chores, I was sitting in Dad's study with Dad writing sentences. I will be so glad to be done with that."

"Sorry about that, sport. And Bryan, you owe me two cookies."

"What?" the little boy looked up in surprise. He tried to look innocent, but he had crumbs on his face.

"You think I didn't see you snitching? You boys run along now." They took off for the playground. Brad took a swig of his coffee.

"He didn't do it," said Jed.

"No time or motive but had to make sure. Wonder who else makes knots."

"Who on earth is going to tie a dropspindle to a shepherd's car with a hangman's noose? Who else would know how to make one?"

"I got no idea, scoutmaster, maybe. You done eating?"

"Yeah, that's the last bite. You gonna eat those cookies?"

"Nah, you take them. I got homework back at the office. You?"

"Heading out to the health food store. Liam wanted to talk. He sounded worried."

Chapter Fourteen

"You've all done so well!" announced Dana in a satisfied voice. "You've spun and plied your yarn, settled it into its shape and dried it, and you're all working on the patterns. Has anyone got any questions?"

"My yarn seemed sort of bumpy. How do I get it to be smooth?"

"It's not unusual for a beginner's yarn to have those bumps. As you practice, it gets smoother. It's still usable and wearable. It might not weave as well, since the looms are so much fussier about that. However, my mother, who is an expert weaver, uses art yarns that have all sorts of bumps and additions, even locks, in her hangings. It gives them depth. I guess, short answer is to simply practice. Most spindles are pretty portable and you can use them anywhere you have a spare minute. I carry one along with me when I'm sitting in a waiting room for something." She reached into her purse and pulled up a short fat spindle. "This is a Scottish spindle, notice how it's shaped? It looks a little like a buoy, and the yarn goes around here, then through these slots at the bottom. The proper name is a dealgan. It's heavy, much heavier than other spindles, and is used mostly for plying. There are lighter versions that are used for regular spinning but they aren't as common. This one was used for plying heavy chunky wool yarn and is larger than most, being about a foot long and weighing in at just under six ounces, and that's heavy for a spindle. Most weigh between an ounce and 2 ounces. I got the dealgan when I went to a Scottish fiber show. Right now, I'm making up a batch of highland wool for use in a vest a friend has ordered for Christmas. I've just started so I've got a ways to go to get the 700 yards she needs. I may use this to ply the chunky wool."

"Where do we get more roving? I mean, I know we have some here, but I'd like to work with some exotics. I've been reading on line about it."

"I'm stocking llama, alpaca, merino, and angora here at Fiber Mavens. You can go online and order just about anything, of course, like camel and yak and picuna. They can get pretty costly. And of course, fiber shows generally have a booth of exotic blends." Dana answered questions, worked with the ladies, and they broke for refreshments and some shopping. Most of the women wanted to get more roving, and some wanted a couple more sizes of spindles. As the ladies were browsing, one of them invited Dana to come to some of the other classes.

Over by the checkout counter, Sophia and Becky were talking with Casey.

"Brad hasn't got any clues who could be using the lost spindles?"

Casey shook her head. "Not that he's told me. We don't talk cases usually."

"That's unfortunate," replied Sophia. "A perfectly good source tied up with red tape. You did hear about the drug store?"

"No, what happened?"

"It appears the spindle felons have hit again. Liam came in this morning and found several things missing and a spindle left hanging on the pharmacy door, which was closed and locked."

"What sorts of things?" asked Betsy as she paid for her roving.

"That's the odd part. They didn't take drugs. They took size large disposable diapers, wipes, bottles, four of them, and three cans of formula."

"Really?" said Casey. "Sounds like a person with a child down on their luck and needing supplies."

"The stuff they took was worth under the amount that would make it be more than a misdemeanor," chirped Annie, coming up to her mom. "I wonder how Liam is taking to being the victim this time?"

"Annie," warned her mother.

"Well, you know, his brother and crazy sister last time did a lot of harm. This time, Liam is a victim and I just wondered," she started but seeing the look on her mother's face, stopped talking.

Sophia nodded. "Yes, that would be odd, to be on this side of the crime this time."

"I'd not wish it on anyone," said Dana coming up. "They hung one of the lost spindles on my truck last week, did you know? They didn't seem to take anything or do anything but scare me."

"Thank goodness for that."

"Still, using a hangman's noose to tie it was a little unsettling."

"Really?" asked Sophia. "Betsy, who would know how to do that? Do we have an executioner?"

Betsy scoffed. "Of course not. We haven't had anyone from here go to the electric chair in a hundred years. It would have to be someone who did macrame or something like that, or learned them like an ex-military person or a scout or something. We have two boy scout troops and one big girl scout troop and a church-based scout troop. I suppose it could be one of the scoutmasters, but you know they all have to be fingerprinted and such to do what they do so don't think it's likely."

"Allyssa, didn't you have a macrame class a few years ago?" asked Jane. "I remember coming to it but couldn't quite get enthused so I let it go. Who else was in that class? Let me think, dear Mildred, but she's passed and that nice young fellow from the paint factory, what was his name? Don't recall and I think he moved away. Rosemary, didn't you take it?"

Rosemary had been quiet up until now. She had stood by her friends' side, just listening. "I did and I still make things. Mostly pot hangers and things for the grandchildren. I've not done any this summer; been too busy."

"Macrame?" came a voice. "Are we going to do macrame after spinning? I used to do that as a child. Heavens, that's been years ago. Last thing I made was an odd wall-hanging for a high school home ec project. It didn't turn out well, sort of off kilter and the skulls on it looked more like, I don't know, something Picasso would do. Anyway, I got a C on it and never did it again. I might like to try it again." Aurora stood next to Casey, holding a shopping bag and a cup of tea.

"Skulls?" repeated Sophia.

"I was going through a goth stage at 15. You know, black eye makeup and fingernails, plaid skirts, hair dyed black. I looked like something out of a horror movie. My mom sent me away to my Aunt Fran's to get straightened out. Fran was a very fundamentalist lady and after a summer of 'you are going to hell if you don't clean up', I cleaned up to get away and come home. That woman could pray the bark off a tree."

"Skulls?" repeated Sophia. "Where have I heard about skulls on a hanging before? Can't place it."

"Well, skulls don't need to be placed. Let's go back to circle and practice. I want to help you all get ready for your next project and smooth some of your yarns' plies." said Dana.

The ladies reassembled. Rosemary seemed particularly quiet this evening, gently letting her spindle drop, turn, and spin the roving as it seemed to magically twist in her hands before dropping down, ready to be added to the spindle, using up the roving in her hand. She thought it soothing and mesmerizing how it seemed to work itself into the proper placement. It almost made her sleepy. It wasn't long and the class was over. She gathered her things, said her goodbyes and walked home.

Chapter Fifteen

"You know if they had come in and asked, I'd have given them the herbs," declared Angelina Carmichael. "I give out samples and such. I've never turned anyone away. There's no need to steal." She was jittery, anxiously filling out the police statement, distracting herself by moving things around on the counter. "I just don't understand people."

"It's a nice little store you've got," replied Jed. "Opened what, last spring?"

"Yes, Heavensent Herbs opened last spring and we carry a full line of everything herb from teas to poultices, to vitamins and herb wreaths – those are a big seller, they smell so good. And live herbs as well, and books and magazines about herbs. And we have our baby corner back here. It has herbs for babies who are teething or colicky, organic cotton diapers, organic baby formula, teething biscuits, things a new mom might need. I came in to be sure the shelves were all stocked and ready and that's when I found it."

She led the way back to the corner. Two sides of the corner contained specific baby and toddler things: diapers, 100% cotton organic, some clothing and baby blankets, and even handmade afghans. There had been a display of a baby in a cotton baby sling. It was friendly and cheerful with a mobile hanging from the ceiling of little soft colorful birds. "I noticed when I came back to be sure everything was stocked, right here, someone took two cans of formula, diaper rash ointment, packaged herbs for colic and fever, two hemp baby blankets and menthol rub for colds. And the display baby in the sling had the drop spindle driven through her chest and she was hanging like that from the mobile. I left it and called right away. It's sickening."

"Seems strange. You've touched nothing?"

"Other than when I stocked it, not since."

Jed took pictures from every angle. He slid the impaled doll into an evidence bag. "Angelina, could you please make me an itemized list of whatever is missing? I need you to finish your statement while I'm checking things out as well. Just go up front, make your statement, just like you told me, write it down, sign and date it, then the next sheet I gave you is for the lost items."

"Why would someone stick a spindle in a doll?"

Jed shook his head. "I don't know. I don't like to not know. Let me call this in while you go up front and write your statement. We will get to the bottom of this. One more thing. Doesn't your brother run the paint factory?"

"That's actually my husband. I got bored, I tried working for my husband and that just didn't work, so I decided to take my herb hobby and start a store. Xavier is fine with it. He helped me get set up and told me it's up to me to make it go, and so far, I'm doing fine. He says he can always use it as a tax write-off if I fail completely. I know, that sounds mean, but he's a businessman right down to his bones. He's been fine with this, happy when I'm happy, but he's not going to be happy to hear about this."

"Well, if happened to my wife, I wouldn't be either. You go write your statement and the inventory list and I'll call this in. We will get to the bottom of this." He noticed her hands were still trembling. "Are you ok? Do you need me to call someone?"

"Oh, no, I'll be fine. It's just I can't figure how they got in. The door was locked when I got here; it wasn't like this when I left last night. I checked out back, I just don't get it."

"I'll check the back door. Do you have security cameras?"

"They aren't completely installed. They're supposed to be done Friday. The man's coming this afternoon."

"Ok. You go write, drink some of your calming tea, and let me check things out. There has to be a way to enter somehow."

Chapter Sixteen

"There!" Alan announced to no one in particular since he was the only one home. "Last online class completed and Monday I start staying on campus all week and coming home on weekends. Sure glad I decided to go to OSU. I can commute home if I'm needed and the way my classes are working out, I can be here on Mondays for work hours at Amanda's office. I'll work Sunday afternoon and all-day Monday, and head back to campus for four days of classes. I can spend Friday afternoons and Saturdays here at home." He got up from his computer and out his apartment door, heading for the back steps that came out in the warehouse by his mom's office.

He heard laughter and paused. "Mom's got that class going downstairs. Gracious! Betsy and Melody must be having a fine time, laughing so loud. Think I'll sneak in back, get a couple of Hannah's cookies and say hello."

He continued down the back stairs and in through the warehouse using his key. He entered the back of the store at the rear of the class. The ladies were up and milling around, chattering as usual. He picked up a chocolate brownie cookie and a macadamia nut cookie and a cup of coffee before he was spotted.

"Ah, HA! Here to filch cookies just like when you were a little kid," declared Melody with a grin. "My land! You've gotten so big!"

"Hi, Mrs. Bibby," he smiled back. "I've been wondering. Can you order text books?"

"I sure can. You need one?"

"I got a list here somewhere and I need it by end of next week for first class. Can they come that fast?"

"I can get them here, I think. If you give me the list and write your number on it, I'll call and let you know what I can get them for, and you see if it's cheaper than the school bookstore. You want new or used?"

"If it's available used, that would be fine. I'd rather buy local if I can. Let me make a copy of the paper on the copier and then I'll give it back. Come to think about it, I need to go buy my lab stuff, too. Good grief, college is expensive."

He took the paper and went in back to his mom's office. He stopped at the door. Annie was slumped on the floor by the office. He knelt down and checked her pulse; she was alive. He took out his cell and called 9-1-1. Then he started yelling for his mom.

Allyssa came running, all the ladies trailing behind. When Casey saw her daughter, she darted ahead. She gently turned her over, keeping her neck straight.

"She's alive, I've called the ambulance," sputtered Alan.

"Annie, Annie! Come on, honey, say something." demanded Casey.

Amanda knelt next to her. She felt for a pulse, pulled open an eye, closed it. "She's been hit in the head from behind, I think. What was she doing back here instead of up front?"

"She took the babies back in their stroller because they needed changed and I told her there was a table right around the corner to change them. It would be more private and better than the ladies room." Casey got up and went over to the stroller then screamed out loud. "The babies! Where did she put the babies? They're not here!"

"What? The babies?" demanded Allyssa. She spun around, her eyes searching the warehouse. Casey ran around the corner and frantically looked around. "Here's the changing pad, she must have been starting to change them when whoever hit Annie came in. My babies are gone!" She ran to the back door which was closed.

"Don't touch anything!" declared Alan. "Let's call the sheriff. We'll just mess up fingerprints if we touch anything."

Casey had her phone out. "Brad, the babies are gone, Annie's hurt, I need you now! Come now! Yes, you heard what I said. Someone took Kai and Enya and hurt Annie. An ambulance is coming." She turned around and looked back, then slowly walked over to the stroller. "And the stroller has a spindle hanging from the handle by a hangman's loop. My God! It has blood on it."

Chapter Seventeen

Jed was at the pastor's house when the call came in. He'd been discussing with the boys and their father the relative merits of putting feral cats into crabby ladies' cars and why that was most likely not a way to advance in school, especially if the lady in question was the vice-principal.

"You do realize they are going to figure out who put the cat there?" asked the deputy.

"It wasn't," started David who saw the look on his dad's face and relented. "Well, ok, it was me. But she was ragging on me and my new sister about hanging out on the playground after school."

"You two were late getting home, but you didn't tell me you'd been getting scolded," said his dad quietly.

"It didn't seem like a good thing to bring up since I already lost us our dessert at supper," he responded.

"So, this time, your little brother came home alone and on time, instead of being accompanied by his big brother keeping him safe. You let a six-year-old walk home from school alone?" demanded his father. "You mom is madder than I've ever seen her."

"That wasn't any reason to give him my pudding." David grouched, his face a study in misery. "And it had chocolate chips in it, too."

"I think you mother would say differently. Now, about your new foster sister; what exactly were you two doing?"

"She wants to be a major league baseball player and I was helping her practice her batting. I'd pitch and you know she can hit anything! No matter if I threw it high, low or outside she hit it. She's amazing! I can't wait to have her on my team at recess," then his face fell. "Well, if I ever have another recess."

"Where'd you get the cat?" prompted the deputy.

"Well, after Ms. Bronson stopped fussing and went back inside the school, we left but we cut across the field to get home faster and we found the cat out behind the grocery jumping up into the dumpster. I caught it and we wrapped it up because it was sort of feisty. It scratched Emory. We thought we were going to bring it home to tame it down but then we thought about the scolding and we both sort of thought of it at the same time. You know Ms. Bronson hates cats; she said so."

"Uh-hum. She doesn't hate cats; she's allergic to cats. She's got to have the interior of her car professionally cleaned. And you thought she'd like a cat in her car, tearing up the stuff in there, trying to find a way out, making messes and spraying all over the inside of the car, did you? Did you not think she'd see you two around her car? She could see you through the window. She caught you red-handed." Jed shook his head. "I guess I've got no other recourse. You've sullied the honor of your badge. I'll have to give it to Brad."

"But I'm one of his irregulars! We have a meeting tomorrow. Brad's bringing brownies and giving us assignments!" protested the boy.

"Not anymore. You can't be trusted to make good decisions, so you're off the team. You'll have to earn it back. Son, you just have to think before you act. Now go get the badge and John, if I can talk to the girl, you said her name was Emory?"

"Yes, she was just placed here last week and she's not been a problem. She listens, she obeys, doesn't talk sassy, and it's not in her records that she's been in any mischief up until now. We honestly thought we had a quiet one this time." The pastor got up and left his office, called up the stairs and Emory came down.

She was a tall, thin child, with a pinched sort of face. Her high cheekbones made her dark brown eyes stand out, and her pixie cut dark blond hair was neatly combed. She wore jeans, tennis shoes, and a sweatshirt that was a little too big. She came in slowly, saw the policeman waiting. A look of panic came over her face for a second, covered up quickly by a look of nonchalance. Jed hated it when kids reacted that way to him. He loved kids, had two of his own, and he hated being scary. He knew it wouldn't do any good to smile. Somewhere in this child's past some cop had done something to frighten her, or some relative had told her to beware, and now here they were. She didn't trust cops.

"Emory, please come here and set down," he said.

"David gave me this to give to you. Why do you need a kids' badge?" she asked as she handed over a metal deputy badge.

"Do you know what this is?"

"A badge from a toy store?"

"No, it's an honorary cop badge. Brad gives them out to kids who seem to be ready and willing to assist the force in keeping the town safe."

"Oh, really?" she replied. "You need kids to protect you here?"

"Really. And they do a great job for the most part. Now, tell me in your own words about the incident with the cat."

"We were just practice batting. We weren't hurting anyone. It was our bat and ball and glove, and everything was fine until this woman comes barreling out of the school and comes over and starts fussing about how we aren't supposed to be here except during school hours and we needed to go home right now. She could have just asked us. She didn't need to yell like that. It was uncalled for."

"Un-huh, what happened next?"

"She stood there glaring and waited for us to leave and then she went back inside. And we started home across a field behind the stores. We found this really pretty, sort of long-haired cat trying to steal food out of the dumpster. David caught it – he's good at that – and I tried to hold it, but it scratched me." She held out her arm and showed them the long scratches, six inches long and deep.

"They must have bled and I'll bet that hurt."

"Well, yeah, but when we got home, I washed them with soap, and they'll be ok. I washed out the tee shirt and put it in the hamper. It wasn't dry yet so it all came out. I've had worse."

"After this discussion, I want you to go to Sally and have her bandage those scratches. There's no telling what was on that cat's claws." Mr. Atherton spoke quietly, "Wasn't she in a dumpster?"

"Yeah, ok. Anyway, David caught it again and he turned around and then this funny look came over his face and he started back for the school. He told me to grab our stuff and I did. And he got to the parking lot and I opened the door and he stuck the cat in and he shut the door and we grabbed our stuff and ran home."

"And she saw you and called us," said Jed. "What you did is called criminal mischief," he said slowly. "And I'll talk it over with the sheriff but David may actually have to go in front of the juvenile judge this time."

"That's not so bad."

"Excuse me?"

"We went in front of the judge when they took my mom away and sent me into foster care last year. The judge isn't scary. Mom will be back in three years and the judge said they'd try to find my dad or my aunt Alinta. They haven't yet so I have to stay in foster care. Both the places I've been have been decent. In the last one, the old lady fell down and got hurt so they sent me here."

"I see. Well, I'm going to write this up. You consider yourself on house arrest for now. You're going to have to at the least apologize to Mrs. Bronson."

"For what? We gave her a pet."

"I don't think that for a moment and neither do you. Don't skirt the truth."

"Emory, go to Sally now." The pastor and deputy stood up as she slumped out the door.

Jed's radio beeped and the dispatcher ordered him to call in. "Got to take this. You ground them both and keep them here, and we'll be back with you."

"Thank you for coming out."

Jed had his phone out and called the station. "This is Jed."

"Jed, get to the yarn store. Brad's kids have been kidnapped."

Chapter Eighteen

The block was cordoned off; the Columbus squad came in and the crime lab people were everywhere, fingerprinting, taking pictures. Brad sat with his arm around Casey, who was pale, hardly breathing, shaking.

"If they don't find them soon, they'll be dead, won't they?" she whispered to her husband. "Or they'll be sold or something. Oh, Brad." Tears started down her cheeks and she turned into his shoulder as he held her.

The Yarn Sisters showed up *en masse*. They were beside themselves. Having gotten calls from the members who were at the spinning class, they had gotten here before the crime scene tape was up and they mingled around in the front of the store talking quietly, making plans. Sheriff Black was in back with Brad. Jed came in and was dispatched back to hold down the fort at the office.

"We'll find them, Casey," said Erik quietly. "I've already called the FBI. You go with Annie to the hospital. Brad and me will work with the guys here and we will find the babies."

The ambulance had loaded up Annie and the EMT came in for signatures. Brad led Casey out to the ambulance and she got in to ride with her daughter.

"I'll come to the hospital as soon as I can," he told her. "I've called the pastors and they've got the prayer chain working. We will get our babies back."

"Brad, the blood on the spindle. They stabbed that doll in the herb store."

"It could be Annie's from her head wound. It doesn't mean the babies are hurt."

"Brad, why would someone do this?" she cried.

The medics came and closed the door. The ambulance pulled out. The last glimpse of his wife was of her holding her unconscious daughter's hand as the door was shut, and then her silhouette in the window. "I don't know, but I aim to find out," he said to the wind.

Chapter Nineteen

"Ok, everyone here," announced the sheriff. "I want you in two groups. I want those who were actually here during the class over there with this gentleman who will take your statements. I need the rest of you to stand over there."

"What's going on?" demanded one of the ladies. "Did someone really take Casey's babies?"

"Are they going to be found?" asked another.

"Are they already dead?" asked a third.

"Separate right now or I am going to go down in history as the man who jailed all twenty-six of the Yarn Sisters. Move ladies, every moment is precious," scolded the sheriff.

The fifteen ladies who had been present moved over by the strange cop from Columbus.

"Now," said Sheriff Black. "All you who weren't here, unless you came here while the meeting was going on, leave through that front door being held open and don't touch anything."

The ladies started to protest. "Leave now or sit in a cell overnight waiting to be processed. This is a crime scene. We don't want any more messing about. Shoo, go. Right now," he walked behind the protesting group of ladies as they were ushered out, and he locked the door behind the last one.

Erik turned around to look at the ladies in the class group. "Ladies, do you remember anyone else coming into the shop while you were in class? Are you certain you are the only ones that were here?"

The ladies looked at each other, alternately shaking or nodding their heads.

"We were on break, and milling around buying roving and such," explained Sophia. "If someone came in out front, I think we would have seen them, but the doorbell didn't ding or anything. We were going from up there to back here for refreshments and talking. Alan came downstairs to filch a couple cookies but he's the one that found Annie. Are we suspects?" she demanded. "That's outrageous."

"You are the only ones that were present. These two gentlemen will talk to you each separately and take your statements. The rest of the men are dusting for fingerprints and trying to find out whatever they can."

"Is Annie going to be ok?" asked Andy. "There was blood back there and she looked so white." Her lower lip trembled and she edged closer to her mother.

Jane Long put her arm around Andy. "They're taking her off in the ambulance to the hospital right now," said Jane softly. "The doctors will do what needs done."

Andy started to cry softly. "We're supposed to graduate together. She's on the cheer team, she can't die."

"Ma'am, why don't I take you and your daughter here together first so you can take her home. Just sit right here by the register and if the rest of you will come back to the classroom, sit down in your circle where you sat before, wait patiently, we'll get around to all of you so you can go home. It's been a trying night," the guest detective spoke quietly as he ushered the group back to the circle. He and his partner interviewed the shaken ladies who alternated between anger, sorrow, and fear. At last, the final woman was interviewed and sent out.

In the back, Allyssa and Alan had been grilled by yet another detective as Brad sat and listened. He watched as the lab workers dusted the stroller, the changing pad, the table, the office, as they took pictures and made soft comments and took notes.

"They had to have been waiting back here," he said quietly. "None of those ladies are capable of doing this. We know every one of them. They wouldn't do this. There has to have been someone back here."

"The back door was locked; there are no signs of forced entry." answered Erik. "Son, why don't you go on to the hospital and sit with your wife? You won't do any good here right now. You can't possibly be thinking clearly."

"I have to find the babies," Brad looked up with a blank expression, so much in shock. "They were just learning to walk. Little Kai would pull himself up to his feet by my chair and beg to be picked up. And Enya was teething and bit me on the foot last night, I had my feet up on the ottoman reading the paper and she pulled herself up, latched onto my toe and that baby can bite! Oh, Lord, what am I going to do it they're lost forever?" He put his head in his hands and started to tremble. Erik put his hand on his shoulder. A detective joined Brad and Erik. "Let me ask you some questions, Detective. You said you knew all those ladies. Is there anyone new in town?"

"Last new person was a foster child. We're pretty stable around here."

"Anyone mad at you or Casey?"

"Not that I know about."

"You send anyone up that might be out and looking for vengeance?"

Brad shook his head.

"Anything odd going on in town?"

"The drop spindle thing is odd, but up till now, it's not been anything like this."

Jed walked over. "Not quite so. Remember my call to the herb shop this afternoon? Wanted to talk to you about that one. Just got back." He outlined what he'd found and showed them the doll with the spindle through it.

The detective from Columbus shook his head. "Somewhere out there you have a really sick cookie. Brad, why don't you go to your wife now. I'll be over to the hospital later to catch you up and will have questions for you both. Concentrate on your little girl."

Brad drew a deep breath and stood up. "I can't help it; everything keeps zipping through my mind. I'm going to ask Matt to drive me. I don't trust myself right now."

"Good idea."

"I'm ahead of you," replied Erik. "Matt and Sandra are outside waiting to go. You just go."

Brad stumbled going outside where he was met by his brother-in-law Matt.

"Listen, I'm going to drive your car; Mom's driving behind us, and I'll ride back with her, so you have a way to get home. We waited for you and Mom's about nuts worrying."

"Thank you. I just don't know what I'm going to do and I don't trust myself right now."

"Understood. Come on, give me your keys and I'll head out. It's only a half-hour drive and you can catch me up. Don't give me that blarney about can't talk about an investigation. This is my nieces and nephew we're talking about."

They got into the jeep, backed out, and were followed by Sandra as they drove out of the town and headed for the hospital.

Chapter Twenty

Toby sat next to Helen as they watched Skye on the playground with some other children playing.

"I think the lunch with your dad last week went well. He's a good man," said Toby. "Do we have everything ready for the wedding now?"

"Yes, but I almost feel guilty having it now."

"What?" Toby looked horrified. "You aren't having second thoughts?"

"Not about us, but with the search going on for the Malcom babies, I don't know. I just wish we could do more."

Toby got very sober. "I know. Brad's one of the best officers I know. I hate that this has happened to them. And once again, we've got FBI and who knows what team combing all over town. It's like the town has been cursed with feds swarming like flies over roadkill."

She nodded. "It almost doesn't feel safe anymore. I almost feel like tucking Skye into the car and having him stay at his grandpa's all the time. Nothing much happens out there where Dad lives. I want to have him with me more now, and with you, but can we actually keep him safe?"

"I'm pretty sure every parent in town is asking the same thing."

"I've got him enrolled in the local school now, you know, and he loves his teacher and he's making friends. You know Mrs. Anderson, the fifth-grade teacher? Her son and Skye have hit it off. They've got a play date after school tomorrow. Aurora and Matt Armstrong are taking them to the Columbus Zoo for a special program and I'm afraid to let him go. I know they're careful. I just somehow can't feel safe." She paused. "Has Casey's daughter Annie come out of the coma yet?"

"Whoever it was hit her pretty hard. I heard the doctors are keeping her in a coma until the swelling in her brain goes down." He stopped a moment. "They're thinking it was someone that she knew. They found the thing she was hit with, some sort of wooden thing. That it could have happened when the shop was full of people taking a class, talking and such, and no one heard anything going on back in the warehouse was pretty stunning, which makes them think Annie knew the person, turned her back to change the babies and was hit."

"Heavy weighted thing?"

"Yeah, I heard it was some sort of spinning thing, let me think. All I can think of is Scottish fold cats, that's not it. Scottish spindle? Maybe. The spinning teacher had brought it to demonstrate something with it, so whoever attacked her must have been in the shop, picked it up, used it, and left it. The Yarn Sisters are beside themselves, blaming themselves for not being more observant."

"I'll bet they are. Now they've got to get involved."

Chapter Twenty-One

Emory sat on the branch above David who was idly skipping stones across the creek behind the parsonage. "We gotta help Brad find his babies," he said out loud. Frowning as the stone skipped only once as it plopped into the water.

"How we going to do that when we're both grounded until further notice.? Since everyone's so busy, they don't have time to see to us and we're stuck here until the adults all talk about what we have to do, so far as I can see, we're going to be grounded pretty much forever."

David frowned. "Yeah. But if we found them, everyone would forget about that cat and everything and we'd be heroes and I bet I'd be back on the irregulars."

"What's an irregular?"

"Brad said an irregular is a soldier who isn't officially on the payroll but does footwork for the military."

"Like unpaid slaves?"

"No, not like slaves. It's fun. We have meetings every couple of weeks and eat pizza and Brad trains us how to do stuff. We went on a field trip to the police academy in Columbus."

"What kind of stuff?" She swung down out of the tree and sat cross-legged, leaning against the trunk.

"Like how to remember things and notice stuff and not to mess up evidence. That last ones important. Can't mess up evidence." he scowled. "And all the evidence is in the fiber store and we can't leave the yard." He plopped himself down under the tree and sighed. "I guess I shouldn't have put the cat in the car. It was stupid. Thanks for trying to back me up."

"No worries." She waited a few minutes. "Your parents are nice, you know? And your little brother isn't even a pain. I kind of like it here."

"That's good. Mom and Dad love about everyone." he paused. "I wonder who that is coming up to the door? Mom's inside, but I don't recognize that woman."

"She's probably someone who wants prayed for or her electric bill paid or something."

He nodded. "We get a lot of company since Dad's the minister."

"What's it like being a preacher's son?"

David had gone very quiet. He motioned her to be quiet and lie down as he watched the lady at the side door. "That's odd. People go to the front door, not the side. She knocked and Mom didn't answer. She's doing the laundry in the basement. Now that strange lady is going in."

A few minutes later, Sally the pastor's wife came out to hang sheets on the clothesline. David ran over to her. "Hi Mom, who was that?"

"That who?" asked his mother as she tossed a sheet over the line and straightened it.

"That woman who went in the side door."

"Nobody came in, David. Hi, Emory."

"Hi, Mrs. A. I saw her go in too. She seemed to knock first."

Sally frowned. "Really? I didn't hear anyone."

She led the way back to the side door. It was open just a crack and they pushed it in.

"Hello?" called Mrs. Atherton. "Is someone here?" Emory ran to the front room just as they heard the front door shut. She jerked it open and looked into the startled face of an older lady who turned quickly and marched to her vehicle and got in stiffly. Emory noticed there were two car seats in the back and the lady backed up and drove off fast. David tried to catch up with her but she left too quickly and he stopped running after her and came back to his mother. Emory turned to find Mrs. Atherton right behind her. Turning around and retracing their steps, Emory and Sally stopped in the living room.

A push pin held a drop spindle hung by a hangman's noose to the wall. Someone had written, "If you look for us, they die," in what looked like marker on the white board by the corner.

"Oh, my Lord," she breathed. "The kidnappers were here!"

"I've got to get Brad," declared David, tearing out the front door.

"Stop, David! Get back here!" called his mom. She had the phone up to her ear. "Emory, don't touch anything! Officer Millie? This is Sally Atherton. I need help right now at the parsonage…"

Chapter Twenty-Two

"That caps it," declared Sophia. "This has taken long enough. We need to get this done. Where shall we meet?"

"Can we all go out to Dana's farm? She has a white board. The fiber shop is still an active crime scene and we can't meet there," replied Melody. She had just been elected as Sophia's new assistant for the Fiver Mavens and was taking notes.

"Get on the Sister's chain and tell everyone to meet me at Dana's at noon with whatever they know," declared Sophia. "I'll call Dana and let her know we're coming."

"What if she's busy?"

"She's a sister now. She wants this to be done, too. Get the word out. I'm gathering drinks and treats now."

In an hour, cars started to show up at the small farm of Dana and Ethel McCallister. Shortly, twenty-three ladies were in the living room where a big white board had been set up at one end, plates of cookies and pitchers of tea set up here and there, and the ladies carrying in their own folding chairs.

"Ladies," began Sophia, "Thank you for coming to the emergency meeting of the Sisters. There is a crisis that we all know about and it has to be solved. Those big city fellows keep wandering around like lost souls and Annie is still in the hospital in a medical coma and Casey and Brad can't leave her. We have got to get the babies back. Now what do we know? Let's put it together. I'm sure we can figure out something. There has to be a pattern to this nonsense."

Jane raised her hand. "We know that 8 spindles were reported stolen and that several of them have been left here and there around town at the scenes of crimes, like someone was trying to copy that patchwork crazy we had a few years ago."

Sophia nodded. She picked up a dry erase marker. She divided the board in two with a line.

"Where were the spindles left? Anyone know?" she asked.

"Are we making another chart?" asked Rosemary.

"Absolutely. Allyssa, you do the honors while I try to remember." Allyssa came up, modified the chart to to be titled *event* and *pattern*, and started to write as the ladies gave the information they had:

1 – David chasing kids around playground with spindle he found.

2 – Hershberger barn fire – a spindle in porch screen door

"Don't forget the one hanging on my truck door," said Dana.

Allyssa wrote: *3 – Dana's truck – Spindle with hangman's noose*

She waited. Andy spoke up, "Annie told me someone had left a spindle in her mom's car when she was on a call, and she gave it to Brad. Nothing had been harmed other than a goat in the back seat, so we aren't sure it had anything to do with it."

"I should imagine a goat in the back seat was enough damage," remarked one of the ladies as they all tittered among themselves. "Casey does get herself in fixes trying to be helpful."

"Focus ladies," said Sophia.

4 – Spindle in Casey's car with no prank except goat

"Angelina Carmichael's health food store, you know, the Heavenly Herb shop, was broken into and baby things taken," said Melody. "I've known her a long time and she was pretty shook up. There was a spindle stuck through a doll like one of those voodoo things and then it was hung from the ceiling like it had been executed. She hasn't got the shop reopened yet. Said her husband was rethinking her working downtown. It's not like she has to work. He was just humoring her."

Allyssa wrote, *5 – Herb shop, baby things taken/doll killed, spindle/hangman's noose.*

"Our pharmacy was broken into," said Marti. "They took formula, bottles, diapers and wipes, baby Tylenol, all things to do with babies and left a drop spindle hung from the locked office door. Baby things again and a hangman's noose!"

Allyssa wrote, *6 - pharmacy, baby thing stolen, spindle left in hangman's noose* and added *baby things* taken to the patterns list.

Betsy spoke up, "And a lot of us were there when the dear babies were taken, and Annie hurt and there was a drop spindle hanging from the stroller that was left and there was blood on it."

Taking a deep breath, Allyssa wrote, *7 – Fiber shop and sisters, babies kidnapped, bloody spindle on stroller.*

"That leaves only one spindle at large," declared Ethel. "You said 8 were stolen originally?"

"No, six we know of, but Rosemary lost hers and David found it, so that's seven, and Annie was hit by the Scottish spindle that I had brought with me as an example to the last class." Dana replied. "So, there could be one more out there."

"Maybe, depends on how you do the math," said Allyssa. "I haven't been in the shop to take inventory. If they can take babies right under our noses, and I know it wasn't any of us, then they can take a couple more spindles to wreak havoc on us all. But let's look for patterns." She looked at the list. "Is there anything else?

Ethel answered, "They all seemed to be leading to something worse each time, at least the ones after the first one. From simple stealing of things to kidnapping and assault. Has anyone heard from Casey or Brad?"

"Matthew told me that Annie is in a medical coma but that they were going to try and wake her up Wednesday, tomorrow. We didn't put dates on any of these, did we?"

"Think back, when was the earliest thing? How far back?"

The ladies agreed all the incidents had happened in the last month. "Ok, so very emergent, 8 things in one month. Does anyone know anyone who might want to do the Malcom's harm?"

There was silence.

"Has anyone got an idea of why someone would take the babies?"

Again, no response.

"The pattern shows they would have been planning this for at least a month – see how they took baby things, baby needs; it must mean they don't mean to harm the infants. However, they might be planning on selling the twins or adopting them out or almost anything, but they have the supplies to keep them for at least a week from what they took. We're on day two of the missing children," said Sophia in frustration. "Is there anything that could help us here?" There was a long pause.

The door opened in the back. "I'm so sorry I'm late," said Sally Atherton. She looked up at the chart. "You need to add an eighth spindle."

"Where?" demanded Allyssa jumping up and taking the marker.

"My house. The kidnapper was at my house this morning. I just finished with the police and they're going all over the parsonage." The room erupted into excited ladies jumping up to hug Sally, ask questions, and the beehive like buzzing got alarmingly out of control.

Sophia finally got their attention. "All right, sit down, calm down. Sally, give the data up here, everyone, we have the last spindle, now what does it mean? Sally, what did they take?"

"I'll start with this morning. The kids were playing in the creek in the back; they're grounded so they can't leave the yard. I was doing laundry and trying to arrange the committees for the Thanksgiving dinner in my head…" She quickly told the story. "And now the entire house is being fingerprinted and examined and John is beside himself and I can't stay long."

There was a pause. Sophia, shaking her head, stood back up. "Allyssa, can you get into your shop yet to do an inventory? If more spindles are taken, we know this person isn't finished. Everyone, is there anyone new in town besides Dana and Ethel? And we can all see there are no babies here, so even if those out-of-town guys are thinking suspicious of us all, we know they wouldn't hurt those children."

"Well, Emory is new, she's a foster child. She didn't have a motive or a means to do any of this stuff, nor has she ever been in this sort of trouble, or really, any trouble to speak of," said Sally, the pastor's wife, her voice soft and a little shaky. "David's ornery, but he'd not capable of this sort of abject evil."

After some talking among themselves, Aurora said, "So no one new, no tourist has been here a month at any of the B&B's, and we all know each other and none of us would get into this. Of course, we never thought that the Clamons would go berserk either, did we? I've heard a bit about that from Matthew. His family was impacted by that pretty badly. And it looks as if someone has singled them out again. The Armstrong's and Malcom's have lived here pretty much their entire lives and I think what happened before was a total a shock to the town. So, it could be someone living here carrying a grudge for some past event."

Heads nodding, the ladies rumbling amongst each other got a little louder.

Sophia took the dry erase marker as Allyssa sat down. "We know it has to be someone who would know how to make a hangman's noose. They had to have some motive. They had to have access. The store was not broken into, so they had to have come in during store hours and hidden in back somehow, and escaped with two babies in a twin carrier, past sixteen ladies and a young man without anyone noticing it, so had to be out the back door which doesn't appear to have been opened. And they are brazen enough to go into a house while people are at home and leave messages. Have I about got it all?"

"No wonder it's taking the out-of-town guys so much time. This is just really difficult." Melody spoke with finality. "Keep your doors locked."

"Wait, I just thought of something," interjected Alyssa. "There is another way into the store. If you go up the fire escape steps, pick the lock, into the upper hallway and down through the back stairs the way my son comes into the warehouse to talk to me in the office, you could get in without being seen. I need to let the sheriff know." There were some murmurs.

"I think we've done what we can," replied Sophia. "Everyone, take a picture of the chart. As you go about town, keep your eyes open and let us know in a group message anything you see. Let's agree to meet back at the store next time. Allyssa, will the shop be open by Friday night?"

"They said I could reopen Thursday."

"Good. We meet there at 6 Friday. As I was saying, keep your eyes open, ladies. We have a kidnapper loose."

Chapter Twenty-Three

Brad sat next to Casey, holding her hand. Casey leaned against the bed, looking for anything, any sign her daughter could hear her.

Brad quietly talked to Sheriff Black.

"That's all we've got so far," Erik said quietly. "Your little girl going to be ok?"

Brad nodded. "They're weaning her off the stuff keeping her under right now and we hope she will wake up on her own by tomorrow., The swelling at the base of her skull has gone down. The tests seem to be coming back good. Her skull was fractured but not badly, and it's already knitting, according to the neurosurgeon. The worst danger is the trauma; she's hopefully going to remember what happened and the shock may throw her back into a coma."

"Doesn't sound good."

"No, it doesn't."

Casey spoke up from her side of the bed. "Don't they say that kidnappings that aren't solved in the first 48 hours don't usually end well?" Her voice trembled and she turned eyes that hadn't been slept in towards him, dark rimmed, red, red veins showing in the white. "There isn't much chance of my babies being alive still, is there?"

"There is an excellent chance. The kidnappers got baby things first, like they were preparing to care for them. Our profiler makes us think that means they had an image of raising these kids on their own, taking care of them, being their parent. They even stole stuff in case the babies might be teething. They got three kinds of formula, and baby food, organic at that, and clothing. We got a report from the ladies at the house church auxiliary that someone had gone in last month and asked for some baby clothes in the correct sizes for twins – and they needed both boy and girl clothing. We're following up on that but they don't keep very good records. The woman donated yarn to the auxiliary in return, a box of it. The ladies said the woman was an older middle-aged woman who said she wanted them for her grandchildren. That's all they remembered."

"Could be our person. No drop spindles?" asked Brad.

"Occurred before they were stolen, so someone was still leaving a hint with the yarn. We have the box but it's pretty unremarkable, too many prints to make any of them predominant. There was one interesting thing though, bottom of the box were some patterns. One of those patterns was for a skulls-on-spiderweb pattern, not unlike a couple afghans from another case, complete with glittering eyes."

"It must be the same person! There aren't any Clamons out we can't account for, the bad ones are in jail or treatment, the ok ones are citizens and none of them match the age of the woman."

"Could have been heavy makeup, maybe?"

"You meet those ladies at the home church auxiliary? Sharp ones, they'd have remembered heavy make-up, Brad paused as Erik continued his information.

"The address she gave as hers is a deserted old shack which we've gone over with a fine-tooth comb. No evidence anyone was there." He stood up. "I need to get back to it. You'll be in my prayers."

Brad looked at his wife. "Honey, I want you to go over there and sit on that side, on the recliner. I'm going to pull the shades shut, and I want you to hold Annie's hand and try to close your eyes a little bit to rest."

"Where are you going?"

"I have a couple ideas I want to try out. Things Erik may not have known. I charged your phone and it's in your purse. I'll call if there are any developments, but I have got to get out there."

Casey stood up to move and he enveloped her in a hug.

"I will get them back, Casey. I swear to God I will."

Chapter Twenty-Four

Brad entered the sheriff's office and saw David sitting in a corner, dejected.

"Hi, David," he said sitting down. "This isn't exactly the principal's office."

"No sir."

"What's going on?"

"I saw the kidnapper and now everyone is over at my house and the sheriff told me to just sit here."

"What?" exclaimed Brad. "You saw the kidnapper?"

David nodded solemnly. "I ran here, and they got mad at me for interrupting and then Sheriff Black came and Mom called and they all took off and here I am and no one has even interviewed me and I might have vital information."

"Do you?"

"What?"

"Have information. You need to report."

"Emory saw it too but she's afraid of cops."

"She was with you?"

"We was by the creek playing. And I looked up and saw this older lady, maybe old like a schoolteacher is old, and she was by the side door. She looked like she knocked but I didn't hear the knock. She opened the door and went in so I thought Mom had called her. But Mom came out just a minute later with a basket of sheets to hang and the lady wasn't with her so I went up to ask Mom who she was and Mom didn't know anything about her. We went inside and there was the spindle hanging on the wall and writing on the wall and the door slammed and then we ran out front and the car backed out of the driveway. The car was a sort of gold brown smaller SUV and the license first three numbers were 43J, and it was an Ohio plate, and there were two car seats in the back but I couldn't get past Mom to take a closer look. The lady looked upset. I couldn't see if the babies were in the seats, but the seats stuck up tall. They were dark colored, maybe blue?"

"Anything else?"

"She was wearing an old lady type dress, kind of red with little flowers all over it. Her hair was that crazy blue white old ladies get and short and curly. She had on glasses." He paused. "I didn't notice her shoes. She had on dress gloves, you know what women wear to fancy parties, short white ones." David screwed up his face in concentration. "The car was sort of beat up but she backed out real fast and took off. And I took off for here to find you and Mom yelled after me and I'm in trouble but I had to tell someone. I didn't think of calling, I just lit out to try and get everyone to chase her down. Mom called the sheriff on cell. I should have thought of that. You know, I think I've seen her at church. I don't remember. I don't pay much attention to the grown-ups there."

"You did really good, David. You've given me some clues. Let's try to find the car. You can go on home now. Your mom is going to be upset enough as it is. Just wait on me, all right? And help your mom."

"Is Annie going to be ok?"

"We sure hope so. Thanks for being observant."

Brad entered the back office and spoke to the researcher. In short order, she had pulled up all older SUV's, gold colored or brown, with license plates beginning in 43J. There were none locally, but one had been reported as missing in Columbus about six weeks ago. In the statement of the man who had made the report, he couldn't remember if he had told a lady he was with if he had given it to her or he had left it somewhere or it had actually disappeared. His name was Charles Alimani and now he was serving time for drug possession. The case, understandably, was on a back burner. He put through a call and reported it had been used in a breaking and entering case here and that was added, the case bumped up and an alert out to watch for it.

Brad checked the case file and found out where the old shack was located. He picked up Rutherford and a couple of the babies' shirts from home and headed out.

Chapter Twenty-Five

Annie stirred. Her eyes fluttered and her pulse went up. The watching nurse spoke to Casey.

"Mrs. Malcom, talk to Annie. She's starting to pull out of the coma and talking to her will give her an anchor to come back up and grab."

"Annie, Annie, wake up, this is Mom. I need you Annie. Come back to me." Annie stirred as if fighting to wake up, she started to breathe faster and deeper and she made a grumbling noise in her throat.

"That's it, honey, fight back! Push your eyes open, you're in the hospital, don't worry about dreams, you're here, I'm here, you wake up." Casey squeezed Annie's hand.

Her head started to move back and forth and she took several deep breaths. Suddenly her eyes opened, and she gasped. "Mom, Mom? The babies? Where am I?'

"That's enough, young lady," said the nurse. "Here, take two deep breaths and swallow a gulp of this. You've been unconscious for five days. Take it slow." She held a straw up to Annie's mouth and Annie took a couple small sips.

"Mom, the babies. Last thing I remember I had set up the table to change Enya and Kai. I heard the door upstairs so I knew Alan might be coming down and I wanted to get them changed before he got there, so I unhooked the seats from the stroller and sat it on the end of the table, and started to unhook Kai, who was fussing, and I heard a noise and thought someone was coming from the class, so I turned. There wasn't anyone there, but I turned back and I felt a crash and I don't remember anything else until now. Are the babies safe?"

"Don't worry about the babies," said the nurse. "You just sip a little water and rest. You've got quite the concussion."

Casey spoke to Annie. "Annie, did you see anyone, anyone at all?"

"What happened?"

"Annie, the babies have been kidnapped. They hit you with something and knocked you out. The police are looking for the babies, but had Alan not come down when he did, you could have died there on the floor."

Annie's eyes were wide open now. "Kidnapped. MY little sibs?"

"We've got the FBI and the sheriff and Brad all out doing their best, but we hoped you'd seen someone or something."

"I just heard a shuffling noise. I saw," her forehead wrinkled. "Man! Thinking hurts!"

"You ought not be trying too hard," cautioned the nurse. "You can't get excited right now, you're still quite fragile."

"I just saw a hand in a glove, a white glove. It was a glimpse, that's all. She had long sleeves. And then my head got hit. Mom, we have to find the babies."

"We are finding the babies. I'll let Brad know what you saw and he'll add it to the other facts and we will find the babies."

"Mom, I'm so sorry. If I'd been more alert, I could have maybe stopped this but I was thinking about a bunch of stupid stuff and I just wanted to get the diaper changed and get back to talk to Andy."

"You couldn't have stopped a determined kidnapper, and you would have been killed and I'd be mourning three children instead of two. You have to rest now; your brain needs rest."

"My head hurts."

The nurse spoke, "I can give you something for that, but we want you to drink some juice. You're on clear liquids for now and you need to slowly wake up the rest of your body. So just apple juice or gelatin for now. Doctor will be here shortly." She left the room to call in her report to the physician, Dr. Michaels.

Chapter Twenty-Six

"Now, now, baby, that's ok, stop crying, I'm getting your bottle warm," crooned the older lady. She brought over a bottle of formula and was dismayed when the little boy spat it out. "Why won't you settle down like your sister? Tommy, you'll never grow big and strong that way. See dear little Sheila? She ate her bottle and she's asleep. Do you have a dirty diaper? Is your tummy bothering you?" She patted the little boy on the back as he struggled and fought her embrace.

"Now, you just need to stop that noise. You'll wake the neighbors," she said sternly. "You'll wake your sister. If you would just take your medicine, you'd sleep so much better." She tried to put a dropperful of Benadryl into the child's mouth, but he spat it out and continued his tantrum.

"All right then, I guess I have to put you back in the closet so you won't wake sissy." She moved over to the closet which was standing open, a baby gate across the front and blankets on the floor. "Maybe you'll be hungry when you get up." She turned off the light and shut the door to the baby's crying. He got louder for a few minutes and then the noise subsided.

The older woman smiled to herself. "It's so good to have you both back," she murmured. "You've been gone so long. I should have realized the government had taken you away. I didn't think for a moment you were dead. That was all nonsense. But we're together as a family again, Jim will be home soon, and he'll just love that you're back." She looked at a picture of her husband that sat on top of a small spinet organ. "Doesn't he look fine in that uniform. He's going to be so surprised at how big you've gotten. Oh, I have my hair appointment. I'll just be sure to lock the door. Getting my hair cut won't take long and the babies will just sleep like angels until I get back. I've got their bottles set up in the fridge and I've got their new outfits laid out for after their baths. I do wish Tommy would get used to the house. It's hard to know what those government agents did to him while he was gone." Putting on her sweater and locking her front door, she started down the front walk.

"Good day, Mrs. Bayou. How are you this fine fall morning?" she greeted.

"I'm just fine and on my way to the shoe store. You weren't at the last class and I worried you might be ill?"

"Oh, no, just busy. I'm on my way to have my hair done, and then I have a full afternoon. I have to admit I haven't been sleeping as well as I usually do but that will adjust soon."

"You're an inspiration!" smiled Betsy. "Always with something to keep you running along. If I ever make it to retirement, I hope I'm at least half as busy. And you garden was lovely this summer: I see you've got it all cut back for winter now."

"Oh, yes, otherwise my mums won't come back next year. Well, good day."

"You, too, dear."

Chapter Twenty-Seven

Brad walked around the small house with his dog Rutherford. The cottage sat back from the road and the description he was given by the Columbus detective about it being a shack didn't fit; had there not been crime scene tape across the front, he'd have thought they'd gone to the wrong address. He moved up closer and walked around the building. It needed paint; it hadn't been lived in for years and the grass was high, but it was structurally sound. Rutherford dashed around, back and forth, front and back and side yards, looking for a scent. He came back to Brad. The back door was unlocked and they went in, saw the evidence of the investigation, and continued to snoop.

They went upstairs and, except for a lot of dust and evidence of mice, it was pretty much the same. There had at one time been pictures on the walls and full closets, but except for a few hangers, there was nothing here. He went back downstairs and walked around, the dog shadowing him, nose to ground. It didn't appear as if this place had been entered for years. He went back outside to the back porch, closed the door and jumped when someone said his name.

"Officer Malcom?" said a deep voice. He turned. Rutherford started to growl, but his tail began to wag, and he sat down.

"Aaron! What are you doing here?"

"I thought I was apprehending a burglar," he teased. "Bishop asked us to keep an eye out on the old place here. Lots of police here early this week, and now yourself, but no one has found anything. I am so sorry about the kinner."

"I appreciate it. Did Amish used to live here?"

"Nay, a widow lady lived here, bereft and sad for many years alone until church folk came and moved her into town. Our women used to bring her a basket of food every couple of weeks. The widow would grow flowers and make arrangements of dried flowers she sold at the old craft store. My wife sees her occasionally in town and she looks a lot better now that she's in among her own folk and not alone."

"I see. So, no one has been here in years?"

"Not until the police all showed up. And yourself. We have you in prayer and hope the kinner are found."

"If you see or hear anything," began Brad.

"I'll call the sheriff's office but this must be a dead end. The lady lives in town who used to be here. Her husband got killed in Vietnam, I think it was. Our Hannah sees her in the yarn shop. She's quiet but always seems to be busy on a project. I think she plays organ."

Brad came off the porch. "Thank you for your time," he said, looking back at the house. "It's actually not a bad little house."

"Nay, it isn't, but the widow won't sell it. Said she might need it someday."

"I suppose that's possible."

Aaron inclined his head and turned to walk away.

Brad walked back to his car and turned back to look again. "Can't help but think there is something here I am not seeing, Rutherford. This used to be owned by Alice and Jim Stoneman. I think I'll find out where she moved to. Let's go, boy." The dog jumped into the back seat and lay on the bench. He whined. He held the babies' shirts between his paws protectively.

"I know, old man. I miss them too."

Chapter Twenty-Eight

Brad came back to the office with Rutherford. He sat down by Erik.

"Checked out the cottage. Any idea about where the lady who owns it lives? Named Stoneman?"

"Name does not strike a bell. Let me look it up. The car the suspect was driving was possibly stolen."

"Marvelous."

"It will show up. How's Annie?"

Brad's phone went off. "That's Casey. Give me a second. We'll both know."

He answered his phone. "Hey. What? She is? Great! Did she say anything" White glove and verified it was a woman. Nothing else? Fine. We're making headway. Keep up your courage. While she's napping, you nap, everything is fine here, I'll be over tonight. Love you, too."

He hung up the phone just as Thom came in. "Brad, got something you need to look at. I think I found out how the babies got smuggled out."

"What?"

"Come on over to the hobby store. I didn't touch anything." Rutherford and Brad trotted beside a visibly upset Thom and made it the two blocks down in record time. Thom led him to the back storage room.

"I don't know why I didn't think about this when all those lab guys were here. You remember when the mess with quilts happened and someone had busted in back here? I locked it up tight except for deliveries. Well, I came down to meet a truck coming in with Christmas stock and found the door jimmied."

"What?" asked Brad. Rutherford was at the door, scratching and pushing.

"Back! Now! Sit! Stay," barked Brad. he went to the door. It pushed open easily. Rutherford whined. "Rutherford is confirming for me the babies were here," he commented. "Looks like they came back here, unlocked it from inside, and came back maybe later that night. Any women in your shop the day of the kidnapping?"

"Several came in to get their husbands and leave."

Brad released Rutherford to go outside to check for smells. He ran back and forth, stopped and picked up something. He brought it back to Brad and sat. Brad drew a deep breath.

"It's Enya's pacifier. See, at the baby shower, someone had personalized a set for them both. It says Enya," his voice got husky. "I'm calling in the lab guys. Would you go shut down the store after they get here?"

"Closed sign is already up."

Brad made the call and in short order the lab truck and four techs showed up and started going over the basement.

"Looks like they were loaded up in back and the car drove off. Are there security cameras back here?"

"Yes, and I pulled the tape from that night but the light was out back here for some reason and it's pretty dark. The shop ladies were all parked over here and entered the shop for class over there. I pulled the tape for the one from the store as well. Hope it helps."

Brad nodded to him. He and Rutherford left the store to the lab techs and walked back to station.

The dispatcher looked up. "Found out that 12 years ago, the women of first church rescued a widow lady from loneliness and moved her into one of the Carmichael's rentals next to Betsy Bayou and her husband. Only one who remembers would be Sophia, I think and maybe Rosemary. They've retired from the First Church ladies' group, but bet they'd recall something like that."

"Looks like that's my next interview."

Erik came in and listened. "Maybe I'll come along. Those women have a way of worming out of someone more info than they give. I want them to realize who's interviewing whom."

Brad nodded with a small smile.

Chapter Twenty-Nine

David and Emory sat next to each other with the police sketch artist working on a picture of the lady at the door.

"She had that funny blue hair old ladies get," he said. "It was short and curly. I wasn't close enough to see her eyes."

"She had on an old lady dress and it was burgundy, and she had on white gloves," Emory stated. "I thought she was one of the church ladies coming to see Mrs. A. She had a big purse. Oh, and a hat, sort of small and tilted on her head."

"Yeah, that's right," said David.

"But we need more details about her face. Was it round or long or skinny or fat?"

"She was skinny," said Emory. "I saw her just a minute before she got in the car, I ran in behind David and Mrs. Atherton and when he took off out the door running for the cops and she turned and looked at us."

"She had glasses," said David. "I saw them as I ran after her and I turned to get Brad. I'd forgot he wasn't here."

Emory nodded. "She did and there were two car seats in the back seat but no babies in them. Her face was sort of thin, and she had wrinkles around her mouth like a puppet, down from her mouth and it was thin too and she had on purply red lipstick. She was sort of hunched over. I just got a glimpse. I don't know what color her eyes were. She was frowning. And her nose wasn't that long."

David said. "She had a black dot in front of her ear, like a freckle, not a tattoo or anything cool." He squinched up his eyes and thought. "That's all I can remember. Her eyes were kinda tilted. That's all. Is it enough?"

"Let's see. Emory, you got a glimpse of her as she was pulling out and while she was walking to her car getting in. You saw her closer up as you were running past, but you both have good memories." The artist kept tweaking. "Is this anything like her?"

Both children looked at the sketch. "I think it's close. Her glasses were sort of not round, more rectangles. Her face was sort of set in a frown like smiling was hard." The artist tweaked a couple more things and finally the children agreed it was close to what they remembered. He sent the picture scan to the computer and made copies to hand out.

"You kids can run home now." said Sheriff Black. "Thanks for your hard work."

"Is Brad here?"

"No, he isn't., He's out looking."

"We can look," started David.

"No, you can go back to the parsonage and stay with your mom. She's pretty shook up. We're trying to analyze the whiteboard but she had gloves on so won't be any fingerprints. You need to help your mom see if she took anything. Now get along and don't dawdle."

David and Emory walked out of the station, none too happy, and turned their steps towards the parsonage.

"All the cool lab guys are gone now," he grumbled.

"Yeah, bummer. It was cool working with the sketch artist though. Wonder if I could do that?"

"Maybe." They walked in silence a few minutes. "I wonder where Brad's looking?"

"I don't know. I don't know him very well. Is he actually a good cop?"

"Sure enough. He's great, comes to school lunch almost every day and visits and if you got a problem, he's there and can help. His wife is a shrink."

"You kidding. The babies belonged to a shrink?"

"Yeah, but Casey's cool. She protects people and stuff. We have got to help get those babies back. I mean, babies are basically worthless but they are sort of cute."

"Babies aren't worthless. They grow up to be real people."

"Yeah, but they're pretty stinky till they know how to use a john."

"You think that old lady is the only kidnapper?"

"I don't know. She seemed sort of mean, you know. And I bet she was strong enough to carry the car seats."

"She left the babies' car seats outside. They found them. She has her own."

"I guess. Let's cut through the cemetery, it's shorter."

"Don't step on any graves, stay on the paths."

"They're dead, they won't care," he replied and took off at a trot. Emory started after him and then stopped a short distance in. He noticed she wasn't there."

"What's the matter?"

"We need to get the cops. We need them, like now."

"Why?" He asked running back. He stopped, looked and shook his head. "Yeah. We need the Sheriff."

Chapter Thirty

"There you are! Hello, baby!" the old woman said brightly, opening the closet door. She carried Kai to the kitchen where his sister was sitting in a playpen quietly sucking her thumb.

"Now, Sheila, you know you daddy Jim doesn't like thumb sucking. You get your thumb out of your mouth right now!" She pulled Enya's finger out of her mouth. Enya's eyes filled with tears but she didn't make a sound. "He doesn't even like pacifiers. And Daddy's the boss."

"Now, Tommy, you sit right here with your sister while I get your bottles ready. I wonder if you're ready for bananas yet? I'll need to get some. Wait a minute, that nice health food store had baby food. Let's see, here's applesauce. Let's try you two with applesauce. I am going to have to get a high chair. I wonder if Finian's has one?" she talked to herself and the babies sat in the pen, watching all that went on. Kai crawled over and sat close to his sister. She leaned onto him. They sat with wide eyes and murmurs soft noises at each other. They noticed everything she did, were vigilant, and stayed close together.

"Now, you two are going to have to start talking soon!" said the old lady brightly. "Here's your bottles, but let's get a diaper change done and then we can have this nice applesauce and maybe a teething biscuit and then your bottles. They're too hot anyway." She took first Enya and then Kai to the side table she was using as a changing table and quickly changed out their diapers. Neither child made a sound.

She settled Enya onto her lap and spoon fed her applesauce neatly, then washed her face off and gave her a teething biscuit from a bowl of them she had on the table. The old lady talked continually as she fed the children. She got Kai and he ate his applesauce without a murmur, but without much interest.

"You seem hot. Are you ill? Do I need to give you some Tylenol?" She felt his head. "You do seem a little warm. Let me just give you some medicine." She sat him back in the pen. It was mesh, the bottom pad covered in a white sheet. There were two teddy bears sitting in the corners.

"Here we are, this is baby Tylenol and let's see, you're just babies so under two, half a dropperful." She drew it up and looked at the dropper doubtfully. "I wonder if half is enough? You're a pretty big little man. I don't want you to get sick and go to the hospital like last time. That was so scary. All those needles and the IV and all. You didn't like that, did you Tommy? I didn't either. And they kept you so long. I thought I'd never get you back. When I saw you in church with that woman from Children's Services, I could not believe it. The government had you the whole time." She gave him almost a full dropper of the medicine and then just in case, gave his sister some as well. She got their bottles, tested them, and picked up Enya to feed. She carried her over to the rocking chair and started to rock her, giving her the bottle, and starting to sing in an old voice, "Hush, little baby, don't say a word, Daddy's going to get you a mocking bird." She stopped a moment and listened.

"No, don't hear Daddy back yet. He'll be home soon and won't that be fine? All of us together again. You know there's a new family in the parsonage, and I have to get my organ music ready for next week. I need to get ready for the choir rehearsal."

She looked at the clock. Enya had stopped nursing and was watching her. She looked around and then said softly, "Mama?"

"What?" exclaimed the old lady. "You called me mama? I knew you could talk. Say it again!"

From the pen, Kai had pulled himself to a standing position. "Daddy?" he called. "Dada?"

"Oh, you two sweeties, Daddy Jim will be so surprised! He'll be here soon. Let's just get you fed and I'll go to choir practice and you can sleep for a while. I never thought I'd hear you say mama so soon." She hugged Enya, sat her in the crib and then fed Kai. She sat him next to Enya and went to get their blankets. The twins crawled close to each other and muttered baby sounds. Enya yawned as did Kai as they lay down next to each other. Enya held onto his shirt and Kai kept his hand on her shoulder as they fell asleep. The old lady came and covered them with a baby quilt, smiling. She checked to be sure the stove was off, picked up her purse and headed out the door, locking it on her way out.

"Hello, Betsy!" she called. "I'm just heading to the church to practice. I want to go over the music."

"That's good. I'm heading back over to the store with my husband's lunch. Been a busy Friday."

"I suspect it has. But it's such a lovely day."

"Is everything ok at your house? I couldn't help but notice all the curtains are pulled."

"I don't want this bright sunlight fading my furniture," she said brightly.

"I suppose that's true. Well, good practice."

"See you at church Sunday!" she called out and marched down the street.

Chapter Thirty-One

The police lab guys swarmed the cemetery.

"It hasn't been dug up," remarked Erik to Brad.

"This is Kai's pacifier. And another spindle. And a shroud like the one in the office. What is going on?" sputtered Brad. He ran his hand through his hair and frowned in frustration.

"I don't know, son. This is a family plot. See, here's the husband, died in Vietnam, April 15, 1970. The joint gravestone for his wife isn't filled in yet. These two little lamb headstones are for babies born June of the year before and dying May 29, the year their dad passed. Whoever the wife was must have been in a world of hurt, losing them so close together. Still, it's been fifty years. She might have moved away or must be in a nursing home by now."

"It's the man who owns the cottage, Stoneman. His wife Alice lives over by Betsy Bayou. She's old and according to all accounts, sort of rattly upstairs, if you get my drift. Plays organ at the church but no one ever actually sees her much, down in the organ pit. She doesn't go to any meetings or anything, pretty much a loner. She had gone to some of the Yarn Sisters meetings but not many, just sort of sat alone."

"I lose husband and kids so close together, I think I'd have been a loner, too." remarked a detective coming up. "No notes. A spindle, the pacifier you identified as belonging to your baby, the afghan. You say there's one like it back at the office?"

"Another case we thought was closed."

"I think it's going to reopen."

"The perps are in jail," protested Erik.

"Doesn't look it."

"Brad, you and me go to Sophia's. I told her we'd be there today at 3 and it's 2:30 now. Let these men complete their work. I'll call ahead and get the file out for the other two shrouds. Let's see, one left at the bank, one left at a funeral, this one at the grave of a long dead hero." Sheriff Black paused. "I'd like to have some experts look and see if they were all made by the same person. Let me call Allyssa and Lydia to look at them in our office."

Chapter Thirty-Two

Sandra Armstrong sat by Annie's bed. Casey had gone downstairs for some breakfast. Dr. Michaels entered the room.

"So how do you feel about going home, Annie?"

"Can't wait!" she replied. "You have a nice hospital but I am really bored."

"Bored is one of the signs you're ready to go home and make your mom crazy until you go back to school."

"When can I go back?"

"No cheer practice for two weeks, but you can return to class Monday."

"Maybe they'll have found the babies by then," she said sadly.

Casey came in and signed paperwork with the doctor. She and her mother helped Annie get dressed to go. They gathered up her flowers and clothes, Bible and tablet. An aide brought a wheelchair in: Sandra went down to get the car. Annie loaded up in the back seat, covered in a blanket, all her things on the seat beside her and they headed for home.

Casey was quiet until they got out of city traffic. "Brad tells me he has some strong leads. He does not think the babies are dead. Erik is sure they'll have them very soon," Casey said out loud, addressing her thoughts to no one in particular as her mom drove.

"If he says so, I think he wouldn't lie to us," said her mother. "I'm just so worried about the little ones. I just don't know. I feel frantic and useless all at the same time."

"Mom, can we drive by the station and ask if there is anything we can do?" asked Annie.

"I'd like to but I think we need to follow the orders. He wants you to be home in bed most the weekend so you can go to school. However, once you're settled in, I'll call and see if anything has happened."

Annie had to be content with that. She watched out the window at the scenery going by, noticing the leaves were all gone down, and as they passed the school, the kids were out at various practices, cheer, football, band. She suddenly missed them all. Passing the museum and fabric/fiber/hobby store, she got a lump in her throat and for a moment started to feel a vise on her chest as though she couldn't breathe. Her head began to spin.

"Mom, I don't feel so good," she whimpered.

"What? What do you mean?"

"I don't want to go back to the doctor but when we passed where it happened back there, and they're all just going on like we haven't lost Enya and Kai, and I could see that hand on the stroller handle again. I felt like I was going to black out, and my head twinged like I was going to get hit again. I don't know."

"That's a delayed memory reaction, honey," said her mother. "Sort of like a panic attack. After you're a little stronger, we'll work on extinguishing that reaction with you."

"Extinguishing?"

"Yeah, stopping the flashbacks. I have them too, or did. I'd pass the store and suddenly be hyperventilating as I think of the babies. I don't know if I'll ever be able to spin again."

Annie was quiet a moment. "How do you do that, stop the flashback, I mean."

"You don't relive it, you go to the place it happened, you force yourself to walk in. In the spinning, you take up the spindle and you spin again. You brain figures out it wasn't the drop spindle that caused all this. Your body accepts the fiber store isn't a dangerous place. You go on. I plan on doing it as soon as we find the babies. I don't want to forget it until my babies are back home. I want to remember it all in case there is something Brad can use to help find them."

Annie nodded. "I think so too. I wonder if we should see one of those hypnosis people? You know, regress our memories and try to think of clues?"

"Hypno-therapists? No, I don't think so yet. Right now, we need rest, both of us. I can't wait to get back into my bed, and neither can you. Brad will be home in a few hours. I'm taking a nap and then I'll make supper."

Annie nodded. She said nothing for the rest of the drive. When they got to their home, they were surprised several cars were in the driveway. The sheriff's wife was standing on the porch with another woman Casey didn't know.

Casey got out of the car and helped Annie.

"What's happening, Mom?" she asked Sandra.

"The sheriff's wives auxiliary came over when they heard Annie was coming home. They were here when I left this morning and told me what they were doing. It appears the police department wives stick together in times of trouble for support."

Casey and Annie moved towards the house, feeling just a little dazed. Women seemed to pop out of the woodwork as they approached the front door and went in.

"Hi! I'm Becky, husband is the chief of police over in Berlin."

"My names Alexis; husband works at Millersburg station."

"Casey, your mom successfully staved off the Fiber Sisters from coming over and running one of their extravaganzas because she knew you'd be too tired. I went through something similar to this when Erik got shot years ago. All of the ladies here have been through the wringer because their husbands are in law enforcement. All we did was the laundry, clean the house, set out casseroles, and make supper. We're going now because you both need rest. You just let us know what we can do to make all this easier."

"Can anyone find my sibs?" asked Annie.

"We've got the best men in the country doing that," replied Mrs. Black. "There's a lot of prayers and a lot of work going on. For now, have faith it will turn out. If there's anything you need, just call. Oh, and the guys in the dining room are there in case the phone rings with …" Mrs. Black's words stumbled. "Well, to be frank, a ransom demand. We think they've been watching for you to come home. They knew you and Brad weren't home, so nothing has come through but pretty sure it will now. We want to trace the call when it comes. Tuck Annie in, and then speak with them a few minutes and then go to bed yourself. Ladies, let's shoo now. They need rest." The ladies gathered their things, and each gave Casey a hug and said something comforting as they filed out, eleven of them.

Mrs. Black was the last to go. "Erik told me they had some promising leads. The FBI is here. Brad's running about with Ruckus and everyone in town has an eye out. We will find these babies," she promised.

Casey tucked in Annie, put a glass of ice water by her bed and shut her drapes. Casey then spoke to the two men with the machines in the dining room, and they explained what would happen if a call came in. Then she went into her bedroom, which smelled of lemon disinfectant, clean clothes, and despair. She laid down on the bed, pulled up the spare blanket, and cried until she fell asleep.

Chapter Thirty-Three

Brad, Rutherford and Sheriff Black knocked on Sophia's door, which opened almost by magic at the first knock. Going inside, they were astonished to find not just Sophia, but what looked to be most of the Yarn Sisters.

"Sophia, what's going on?" asked Brad mildly. "I thought we were going to talk about Mrs. Stoneman."

"We are. We've just been gathering facts. All of us want to help. We have to find those dear future knitters."

Sheriff Black raised his eyebrows. He looked at the living room and the fifteen ladies waiting for him.

Sophia plunged ahead. "Now we've been gathering data about Mrs. Stoneman. Susie over here got into the microfiche at the newspaper office. Mrs. Stoneman married Jim in her junior year of high school; they set up housekeeping in that dear little old cottage out in the boonies. She was pregnant and didn't realize it when he enlisted and went off to Vietnam. He was hoping to use the GI bill to get a college education when he got back. Except, he didn't get back."

"We knew he got killed in Vietnam," said the Sheriff.

"And she went ahead and had twins. A little girl and boy and their names were Sheila and Thomas," said Hannah. "She had them in the hospital in Loudonville. Our hospital was only a clinic back then."

Sophia continued, "She was just 18 years old when her world fell apart like a jigsaw puzzle knocked off a table. Her husband killed, she got the flag delivered to her, all of that, she was alone. Her mom babysat the babies so she could work. It wasn't easy. There wasn't much welfare in those days and it took six months to get her widow's pension from the military and she couldn't get the social security pension because she was military. Once her pension came, she stopped work so she could stay with the twins. The babies were greatly loved and cared for, but they both came down with teething colds that somehow went into bronchitis. She took them to the hospital, but they died a few hours apart." Sophia leaned back in her rocker and took a long breath.

"Alice came unglued," Jane Long took over, nodding at Sophia. "The ladies in the Auxiliary back then interviewed people who knew her and were told she went into seclusion at that little house. She gardened, she stayed to herself, alone, and no one could reach her. Then the pastor before Pastor Primo made a visit, was horrified at what he saw, and insisted the church ladies get involved."

"I was there, I was just a young mom myself," said Sophia in an important voice. "Mildred and I took her under our wing. We found out she could play organ and we got her hooked up to be the church organist. Betsy's husband found out the little house next to us was up for rent to own, and we all convinced her to move into town. We all sort of took care of her all these years."

"And that's why we just don't see how she could be the kidnapper. It doesn't fit. She's very quiet, she plays organ for church and Sunday school, she doesn't say boo to anyone. Even when she comes to yarn meetings, she sits quiet and doesn't talk, just knits and learns and sometimes will drink tea."

Then Rosemary spoke up. "But I think she knows something about it. I've been in her house. It's always clean, she has food but she makes these really weird afghans, with skulls in them, and ghosts. She has a sort of shrine set up in the hallway. It has the flag she was given in a box in front of Jim's picture, she has pictures of the babies on each side and booties that were theirs. She keeps candles burning on that table. The table has one of her spooky shawls on it. I have suggested she go to a grief counselor."

Brad nodded. "Have you heard anything that would make you think the babies are at her house?"

"Well, that's the bad thing. Do you remember we told you about someone who came to the church asking for some baby things a few weeks ago? The ladies in the Auxiliary now are all younger and they didn't know her. We talked to them though and she seems to fit their description of Mrs. Stoneman."

"Really?" asked Brad.

"And we checked a little further and found out that when she was in high school, she got in trouble a couple times for shoplifting. Her parents were glad when she found Jim and consented to the marriage before she was 18 because it saved them a bunch of trouble with the court and someone else would be in charge of keeping her in line. And her dad helped Jim buy that little house just before he left for Vietnam so she wouldn't have to worry about rent. Jim just sent the payment to her dad each month."

"I see," said Erik.

Brad spoke, "Isn't Alice a little old for doing something like this? If she got married in 1968 at age 17, she'd be nearly 70 years old right now."

"That's just it, Brad," replied Betsy. "She's usually so quiet, I hardly hear her coming and going, and suddenly she's smiling at me, all perky, waving and saying good morning. It's like a total change has come over her. And why has she got car seats in her car? And where did she get that car? She hasn't driven in years."

"What?" gasped Sophia. "You didn't tell us about that. I thought it was the same car."

"What?" asked Betsy.

"Back when she was at her little house, she had an older gold colored car. I don't know what kind. I didn't realize this wasn't the same car. I've seen it sitting in her driveway but didn't think anything of it. Why didn't you say it just showed up?"

"Couldn't get a word in edgewise with all you talking," replied Betsy. "I do think she could do this. She's strong, she isn't quite right upstairs. I don't think she'd hurt the babies but if she does think they're hers, she could have them in the house as we speak."

Brad looked at Erik. "Is that everything?" Erik said quietly and looked around.

"Just that Brad's babies are the same age hers were when they died in the hospital. They were taken in by ambulance. She had car trouble and couldn't get there until the next morning and she never brought them home. They died the day she arrived. She never got to say good-bye to them." The ladies in the room were very quiet. "I talked to her brother in Houston. He hasn't seen his sister in years but said they've tried to get her to talk to someone but she never would. He was glad she was moved into town. He said she would visit the old place now and then. She'd never go to the cemetery to visit the graves, though, as if she thought if she didn't go there, it would make it less real."

Erik cleared his throat. "I'd appreciate his address. Thank you, ladies for your time."

Getting back into the car, Brad said, "I'd like to go visit Ms. Stoneman. I want to ask a few questions."

"I would as well. FBI ran her through the data base and she hasn't got any record to speak of. No reason to talk until now."

"I think I have reason now." said Brad firmly as he started the squad car.

"I'm having Jed meet us there. He'll be at the back door."
Brad nodded.

"We need to look as if we aren't breaking land speed records, Brad," said the sheriff gently. The speedometer slowed. Erik rolled his shoulders back.

They got into town, drove the few blocks to the Stoneman house. Brad got out and he and Rutherford walked up to the house door. The dog tilted his head, he stuck his nose by the door sill and whined. He started to scratch at the door.

"Cars not here." remarked the Sheriff. "I'm not sure we've got enough for a warrant."

"Call Judge Milo anyway," said Brad in a soft voice.

"He'll ask me why we haven't got the FBI with us if we're so danged sure."

"We can tell him they're following leads." Brad had his ear to the front door and Rutherford got more agitated.

Jed called them. "Erik, neighbor to the left said she left the house carrying two bundles and headed out an hour ago. I don't think anyone is home."

"Can you see anything from the back door?" asked Erik.

"No, curtains everywhere. Neighbor said he thought he heard a baby crying a couple days ago but nothing lately." Brad tried the door. It was locked.

Erik was on the phone, carefully explaining to the local common pleas judge why they needed a warrant.

"We have probable cause," he told Brad. "No, don't break the door." He went over to the railing, lifted a pot and handed him a key. "Most the older ladies leave a key under a pot on the porch. She's no exception."

"If the thieves knew that, it could be a problem."

"It was a thief who told me and it does not matter to the old ladies."

The door opened, with Rutherford eagerly pushing ahead. He dashed around the apartment whining, bringing back a baby blanket.

Erik and Brad hustled through the house, then called the FBI lab team.

"The babies have been here, and not long ago," declared Brad. "The baby bottle over here is still warm, the diapers were changed and left."

"There's a baby bed in the closet," said Erik quietly. "And here's that shrine but the pictures are all wrong. Brad, this picture is of you on patrol. These pictures are the twins. What on earth is going on in this ladies head?"

Rutherford had come over, sniffed the bed, had jumped into the playpen, ran from room to room and stood by the laundry room door on the side whining to get out.

"We've got to find her before she hurts the kids," declared Brad. "Rufus! Come on boy, what direction?"

Brad opened the door; Rufus ran out, nose to the ground casting about the yard, came to the side yard and started to bay. Brad ran over. "Tire tracks. She must have brought the kids out in the back, loaded them in the car here, and driven off. Which way did they go, Rutherford Ruckus, which way?"

The dog ran to the street and started to run down it, full bore, nose to the ground, ignoring traffic and distraction. Brad ran after him, keeping him in sight. Erik watched in frustration until the lab people showed up.

"I think I just saw your detective running hell for leather down the back street. Is he high?"

"High on hope," replied Erik. "The babies were here. Jed, be liaison, you guys find out what you can. Judge has a warrant coming. I'm heading out for Brad."

Chapter Thirty-Four

"You children are being so good," cooed Alice as she drove slowly towards her old cottage. "I don't know what is holding back your dad from coming. He's usually home by now but we need a nice outing. Such a lovely day out."

Kai and Enya sat quietly in their car seats. They looked feverish. Mrs. Stoneman stopped at a stop sign and waved at a boy who was standing on the corner with his bike waiting to cross. A thin tall young girl was with him, also holding up a bike. David's eyes widened.

"That's the sheriff's kids!" he exclaimed. "I've got to tell Brad. You follow them."

"And what do I do if they stop?" she asked practically. "You think a kidnapper is going to listen to me?"

"Here, take this. It's Mom's cell phone. She lets me carry it now to call her if I get into trouble."

"So, who do I call if I get in trouble?"

"You call 9-1-1. I've got to go. Go, now, don't let them get out of sight!"

David sped off towards the police station. The foster child looked at the phone and hopped on her bike, sticking the phone in her pocket and heading after the car which had not turned but wasn't driving fast.

"I sure hope she hasn't got a long way to go. I'm pretty tired already. I could just tell them she out sped me." She peddled as fast as she could on the old bike.

Shortly, she was overcome by Rufus charging past her. A few yards behind, Detective Brad was pumping his legs as fast as he could.

"Officer, we saw the babies in a gold car, a little one, they're in back and she went that way. Take my bike. You'll make better time!" she said, stopping and jumping off.

"Thanks, that car up there?

"That's it. You better get there before Rufus or he'll tear her up."

"Not as fast as I will!" Brad tore down the street on the bike after Rufus.

Soon after him came the sheriff's car. He stopped and picked up Brad. They tossed the bike in the truck. And headed off the way Rufus was baying, windows down.

"I wonder what all that noise is?" said Alice to the babies. She pulled into the church parking lot. "Wouldn't you know it; I've left my keys and can't get in to practice. "What are you babies back there for?" she seemed confused. "Oh, I promised to let you see your daddy, didn't I? Well, we can go visit for a few minutes. Pastor Matthews will be here to let me in shortly. He's been such a help since Jim passed. I can't believe it's been so long." She got out of the car, took up a small bouquet of flowers and took the babies out of the car seats. Tucking a child over each shoulder, she stumbled slightly, walking towards the cemetery.

Chapter Thirty-Five

Sophia stepped outside on her porch, shading her eyes, listening.

"I do believe that's Ruckus," she said to the ladies behind her. "He's got a scent."

"Maybe it's the babies!" exclaimed Betsy.

"But that's coming from the direction of the church, not your place." answered Sophia.

"Maybe we ought to go find out what's going on?" suggested Jane.

"I think we best not take too many cars," answered Sophia. "Let's just carpool over." Shortly sixteen ladies were packed into four cars, hurrying to the church.

Casey and Annie pulled up to the police station. Annie drew a deep breath. "I can do this, Mom. I can go in and make a statement and I can come back out." Her mom nodded as they got out of the car just in time to have David Atherton crash his bike in front of them.

"David, what on earth! Are you alright?"

"I saw them, me and Emory together." He gasped, panting hard. "She's following the kidnapper. She's got mom's phone. I got to get the sheriff."

"Where? Which way?" asked Casey, pulling him up.

"Listen!" declared Annie. "That's Rutherford! He's got their scent!"

"Let's find help and follow him!" declared Casey. She ran into the police department.

"Listen to David, then send anybody out after Rutherford, she gasped and ran out.

Millie looked up to see the front door slam. "I was going to tell her the sheriff is already in pursuit, but I got the feeling she's going to be as well," said Millie. "Still, David, let me get you a drink and you tell me what you saw." She pulled a cold bottle of water out of the fridge and said, "Now I might not be able to type as fast as you talk so bear with me. Tell me exactly what happened."

Taking a deep breath, David started his tale.

Chapter Thirty-Six

Rutherford ran panting up to the church, sides heaving, and waited for his master. The gold car was sitting in the parking lot. Rutherford Ruckus waited for Brad to pull up and get out of the car. He knew his training, but he was impatient. The puppies were here, he could feel them, and something was wrong.

Brad stopped, parked and he and Erik jumped out.

"Church is locked," said the sheriff. "Choir won't start for three hours. Pastor's on his way over to open it if needed."

Ruckus whined. He got up and started off at a lope across the parking lot and around the church to the cemetery. Brad went after him, unfastening his holster and slowly pulling out his pistol, Erik following a short distance behind, waiting for the pastor, but ready to rush if needed.

Up ahead, Ruckus howled a greeting. Brad ran, disregarding all his mother ever told him about stepping on graves. He arrived at the Stoneman family plots. There, sitting in their car seats, Enya on Sheila's grave, Kai on Tommy's, sat his children. They looked at him and started to cry softly. He unfastened them both and hugged them. He felt their fevers, and their listless bodies and knew there was a problem. Erik puffed up. He spoke softly. "Ambulance?"

"Absolutely. Lab guys as well."

An old lady was sitting on the ground behind her husband's gravestone, wrapped in a shroud, using a drop spindle, making yarn, humming to herself. The shroud she made was unfinished; as she got several yards of yard made, it appeared she crocheted it into the pattern until she'd used up one bit and went back to spinning.

"I told them you'd come, Jim," she spoke. "We meet here every Thursday afternoon after I practice, and I told them you'd come so they could see. I've just about made enough yarn for me to make my shroud and when it's done, I'm going to be joining you in heaven." She smiled up at Brad, holding his babies. Rutherford sat between she and Brad, growling softly under his breath. Black shrouds enveloped the car seats.

"Mrs. Stoneman," began the Sheriff. "You are being arrested on a charge of kidnapping. You have the right to remain silent. Anything you say can and will be used against you in a court of law. You have the right to an attorney. If you cannot afford an attorney, one will be provided for you. Do you understand your rights?"

Alice looked confused. "I don't understand. Who was kidnapped? I brought my children to come see my husband. They need to get to know him; he's been away a long time."

"Mrs. Stoneman, these aren't your children. They belong to Casey and Brad Malcom. They've gone about crazy trying to get them back."

"Who are Casey and Brad?"

Erik looked at Brad. "Did you call for an ambulance?"

Alice scrambled to her feet. "No! No ambulances! That's how I lost them the first time. The ambulance came and they took them away and I've been alone so long. God gave them back to me and you aren't taking them away again! We're going to be all together once more and forever," She ran at the sheriff, waving her spindle at him like a sword. "I said no ambulance!"

Rutherford hit her mid center and knocked her over. He stood over her with his teeth bared, a low growl in his throat.

Suddenly, sixteen ladies from the Fiber Sisters showed up and started fussing.

"Get him off that lady! Stop that dog!" demanded a couple.

"Brad, I thought Ruckus was a gentle dog? Why is he attacking Alice?" asked Sophia, trying to go to her friend.

Annie and Casey came running to Brad and shortly Casey had the babies in her arms. Brad turned to Rutherford.

"Ruckus, let the sheriff get the cuffs on her and then let her up," he directed. "As for you ladies, this woman kidnapped my children and I think they're sick. I don't think she's completely in her right mind, but she also tried to attack the sheriff with a spindle. And I am calling an ambulance. My kids have fevers."

"No!" screamed Alice. "Not again! They aren't sick! There won't be any hospital this time. They're going with me to heaven with Jim!" The Fiber Sisters got very quiet.

Sheriff Black had Alice handcuffed.

"Heaven?" asked Sophia. "Alice, what are you talking about?"

"I have their shrouds. They'll go to heaven. I don't have mine ready yet. Jim's has been stolen, but I know he's watching us. He must have taken it. It was so pretty."

Brad came over and swung Alice around. "Heaven? They're too young for heaven."

"How were they going to go to heaven?"

"They were just going to go to sleep and so was I, but I needed to get my shroud done first so we could find each other in heaven. We'll all have matching shrouds."

A strange look came over Brad's face. He pulled out his phone. "On the ambulance, hustle it up. I think my children have been poisoned."

Erik was on the phone with the lab guys, who were back at Alice's house. "That's right, look for poisons, something that could kill toddlers, something added in food or milk. We're heading to the hospital. Meantime, get someone here to take this felon to jail and book her on kidnapping and attempted murder."

The Yarn Sisters were quiet. For once, they could not think of a thing to say. The pastor's wife took Sophia's arm and started to lead her back to the church. "It's time we went and let them do their work. The babies are with the parents. It's time we left," she said softly. Numbly, the ladies all followed Sally back to the sanctuary, where they sat quietly. Some prayed. Others just sat.

Finally, Sally stood up. "I know this has been a terrible shock. I know our hearts hurt, but it could have been so much worse. Had it not been for the diligence of even our youngest members, this could have ended much worse. As it is, the babies are home, the perpetrator will get the help she needs finally, and we can go into the holidays with a grateful heart that all is finally well in Lyonsville. Shall we pray a moment and then go to our homes?"

The ladies stood and Sally led them in a heartfelt prayer that gradually got them back into themselves.

Chapter Thirty-Seven

The babies were admitted. Alice was screened, given an antidote, watched for 12 hours, and sent to jail.

Brad stood between the babies' beds with his wife. Casey and her mother sat in chairs waiting. The babies slept. The hospital had pumped their tummies, filled their stomachs with a charcoal slurry, and done bloodwork. They were not out of danger yet.

Dr. Michaels had called in a pediatric specialist. They'd gotten the results of the tests and were just about to enter the room when Helen and Toby came up. The specialist asked, "Nurses, would you both come with us? It would be good for the family to have some support right now."

"It's going to get a little crowded in there."

"Better crowded than empty in this sort of case," replied the specialist.

They knocked on the door and Dr. Michaels led the way in. "Good afternoon, Mr. And Mrs. Malcom. This is Dr. Fieldlings. He's a pediatric specialist from Dayton who came up when I called. I've asked him as he has done a lot of work on this sort of problem and I wanted your children to have the best chance of full recovery."

"Thank you." replied Brad. "What's going on?"

Dr. Fieldlings started. "It appears the neighbors never heard the kids because from day one, she was both isolating them and drugging them with mild barbiturates and too much Tylenol. We've put activated charcoal in their bellies; we're flushing their bodies with IV fluids, and we're watching for symptoms. When they were brought in, their level was high, but it's come down considerably over the last few hours. The largest danger was seizures and respiratory problems, but those have not happened.

"We won't know if there is lasting neurological damage until a few days have gone by and they've been under observation. I would like to do an EKG and ECG on the children while they are still semi-conscious to get the best readings, but there's a good probability they're going to be ok. I don't expect them to wake up for another couple hours, so we're going to take them down for tests now.

"If those exams come back well, and they wake up in the next three hours, and their bodies seem to have eliminated the drugs in their system, then they'll be able to go home in, I'd say, 48 hours. If not, we may have to take them to Children's for more intense care. The next couple hours are crucial. We want to try and eliminate long term effects of the drugs and avoid seizures. In the meantime, the bloodwork showed some interesting factors.

"Whoever had the children was feeding them not only over the counter prescriptions but appeared to be giving them some herbs. She most likely thought it would make them healthier. The police found a couple bottles of herbal complex they sent over and the babies tested positive for it and for CBD oil. From what we were told, she was not completely in her right mind. It's almost as if she was playing with dollies, we found evidence she'd put Band-Aids on non-existent cuts, given Tylenol for non-fevers, used too much toothache gum ointment, that sort of thing. Whatever was wrong with her, it's a good thing you got them back. She could have damaged their livers.

"At any rate, we're going to run tests over the next couple hours; we're pushing fluids, and we hope they regain consciousness without seizures within the next three hours or so. If we can get them over this hump and get the drugs all out of their systems, they ought to recover."

"Her elevator never left the basement," growled Annie.

"Shh," cautioned her grandma.

"If everything goes well, and nothing is damaged, they could be home in two days?" Brad clarified.

"That's what my prognosis is right now. With your permission, we're going to move them down and start testing. If you want to come down, you may, or you can wait here for them to come back."

Casey spoke first. "I'm not leaving them."

"I'm not either," said Brad.

Sandra stood up. "I think I need to get Annie and myself home. She has to get strong enough to go back to school, but you call us if anything happens, ok?"

"I think I may have left Rutherford with the sheriff," said Brad. "It gets fuzzy after the ambulance came."

"Ruckus is with Matthew over at the hardware. He's coming to the farm tonight. I'm taking Annie home and staying there with her and Ruckus. You take care of my grandchildren, you hear me?" she said as she hugged Casey.

"Yes, now that they're back, they're not going to be left for a second," said Casey.

The cribs were unattached to the wall, the nurses pushed them out and down to the elevator, Casey and Brad followed. The babies never moved, lying attached to their IV's, still, pale, and breathing slow. Sandra and Annie got on another elevator and headed for home.

Chapter Thirty-Eight

The room where the Christmas tree stood was covered in ripped-off wrapping paper. Rutherford was lying on his back, snoring in a corner. Casey sat next to Brad on the couch, sipping hot cocoa. Annie was on the floor with the twins. Matthew, Aurora and Skye sat on the floor, assembling a Lego car.

Casey sighed. "I can't believe six weeks ago we were bereft of our babies, all due to a crazy old lady. Brad, I ever get that nuts, just shoot me, ok?'

"I promise." He paused. "I heard the other day she was declared incompetent to stand trial and has been placed in the mental hospital south of Columbus and will stay there indefinitely to life. If she becomes competent, there's to be a plea bargain. The Fiber Sisters are still shaken by what happened that one of the ladies in our town should be so ill and no one noticed."

"I know. There's a good reason we ought to look after our neighbors. After the holidays, Allyssa has called a meeting with the ladies to get everyone back on track."

"That's not a bad idea. Now that it's over, and the babies are fine, it's all really sad. I hope nothing like this ever happens again to anyone in our town." He paused a moment. "Of course, there is one unsettling thing about all of this."

"What's that?"

The shawl that was hung up in Finian's and the one hung up in the bank don't match the ones Alice made. Several of the

Yarn sisters looked t them for us and declared they'd not been made-Alice crocheted. Those ones are knitted."

"She didn't know how to knit?"

"Not that anyone remembers."

"So, you're saying there's a crazy person left out there?"

"Possibly." She sighed.

"Well, for now, we have each other together, in our own home, and safe. We have so much to be grateful for this Christmas."

"I agree, but the greatest thing to be thankful for is each other," he smiled in satisfaction. "Wonder if those two are going to make it official soon? Skye sure has taken a shine to Matt."

"I was sad to miss Toby and Helen's wedding," Casey sighed.

"Babies were still in the hospital, they understood."

"Still, I love weddings."

Sandra looked up. "I have a sort of surprise for us all," she said. "It's a trust me trip. We have somewhere to go."

"Excuse me, mom?"

"Everyone get their coats on and Casey, we can go in your van, and Matt can carry any extras. We have somewhere to go."

Shooing everyone out into the hallway and getting them all dressed in coats and mittens, they loaded up and Sandra directed the way out of town. It was a beautiful Christmas day.

She directed them to Dana's farm, where they found several other cars already arrived.

"What on earth is she doing on Christmas day?" Casey exclaimed

In the doorway of the barn, Alan Martin was directing people.

"It's an old custom with the McCallister's. You'll see when you go inside," her mother stated.

Following the others, Brad saw Erik and his wife ahead of him, several of the Yarn Sisters, the pastor's wife.

"Isn't it wonderful?" Sally enthused. "Wish we had had this at our Christmas Eve service."

There at the end of the barn, using a stack of hay as a backdrop, was a live nativity. All of the animals in the nativity had a baby at their side. Local teens played the parts of Mary and Joseph, the wise men, the shepherds. It was a marvelous tableau. Soft music played and a recording of the chapter of Luke about the birth of Christ repeated itself.

After watching for a few minutes and exclaiming over the baby animals, they followed the crowd outside and to the back porch where refreshments were being given out: hot cider, warm cookies, and coffee. Next to a nicely decorated Christmas tree, Dana was handing out small fiber gifts for Christmas, 3-D printed drop spindles, small bags of roving, felted laundry balls, stocking hats, beaded stitch counters, and for the less craft inclined, calendars featuring pictures of the farm and the animals.

Dana was greeting all her neighbors; people were getting acquainted. "I had planned on doing this last night but heard it would interfere with the church Christmas Eve services, so decided to do it today," she explained. "We're only going to be open for a couple hours so please sign our attendance book. It's been so much fun meeting you all." She smiled as she shook hands and wandered around. "The workshops are open in my barn for those of you who want to see mom weave on the big loom, and we're so glad you came."

"Do you have a petting zoo?" asked one parent.

"No, it may seem like it, but not really. However, if you follow Molly here into the side barn, we have some animals that enjoy petting. If you take one of these bags of carrot and apple slices, you can feed them," answered Dana, handing out bags.

"There goes Molly with another group of kids." Dana smiled at Casey as she came up and got bags to feed the animals.

Sally came up to Casey and joined her on the walk to the second barn. "Emory's family was found and she left our home three days ago. I got a call from her last night and she's happy and having a good Christmas with her uncle. He hadn't even known there was a problem or that she was in foster care!"

"People can be heedless even of their relatives, I guess." Casey went over to pet the highland calf in the barn.

Brad and Casey, Annie and the others stayed an hour or so, and left to go home.

"I'm glad she wasn't made upset by someone using her spindles for crimes," remarked Brad. "I wonder if she's going to teach anymore."

"That's something the fiber ladies and Allyssa are working out in January. I hope so. I want to get back to it; I find it soothing and it's something I can do with the babies around."

"Merry Christmas, dear."

"You too. Let's get home so I can make a feast. And honey, thank you for the spinning wheel. I can't wait to learn how to use it."

"Why wait?" asked Annie. "You can pull it upon You tube this afternoon."

"Maybe, but I'll wait for the class. There's something good about getting together with friends to learn."

The Malcom's got into their car and started for home, soft Christmas carols playing from the CD. As they pulled into their house, it started snowing again, and they all went in to relax and just be thankful to be home and together and safe. Ruckus took his place by the babies' cribs and closed his eyes as wonderful smells started coming out of the kitchen.

Thank you for reading <u>Criminally Spun Out!</u>

Our Next Cozy Mystery Series is called **The Furry Family Mysteries**, and this is chapter one of book one, just to give you an idea of the fun to come.

Chapter 1

Hazel stood on her front porch overlooking the comfortable row of mid-fifties houses. The street was quiet at this hour: too early for school buses, too early for commuters, just a few walkers and joggers going about their business getting up a mild sweat before they started their day. The newspaper carrier tossed her paper up to her, and, as always, her dog Ascot jumped up and caught it and fetched it to her. Ascot – a Cavalier King Charles Spaniel with long, soft ears, big eyes, black, brown, and white coat – sat down next to her watching the people, perfectly content to be her companion on this brisk morning.

The newspaper boy tossed the paper onto the porch of Hazel's next-door neighbor. Lillian heard it and came out, followed by Minuet, a sunburst Persian, who lazily wandered out the door, tail high, nose up, owning the porch. Ascot sighed and lay down to avoid seeing her and barking. It wasn't proper to bark at your master's best friend's idiosyncrasies; that being that she was, to put it gently, a cat lady. Ascot's owner was a dog lady. How they came to live next to each other was a total mystery to Ascot, but he'd ask Freddy, the retired police dog. Fred had been here longer than anyone else in the household.

"Morning Lillian, lovely day, isn't it?"

"Just perfect for late spring. My crocuses are up all over the yard, I have some almost-up daffodils. I'm going to open up the outside runs, if that's ok?"

"I'll be having the dogs out for their morning walk shortly. Just let me get them all attached and we'll be on our way."

"Good! I want to do a good cleaning while the animals are out. The poor dears really hate the vacuum. My niece is coming over to the meeting today. So nice the library allows us to use their ready room downstairs."

"I've got the thumbprint cookies ready and boxed, waiting."

"I got some of that delicious chocolate mint tea they just got in over at Mileson's. It ought to go well. Do you know if Amelia has the agenda typed up for us?"

"I don't, but she's so efficient she probably has today's and the next three months as well. I'll see this afternoon. Do you need a ride?"

"I have to go shopping this afternoon, so probably not." Both ladies were too polite to mention that when they rode in each other's cars, neither household of cats or dogs could stand the smell that got on them and would be very standoffish, especially the two Siamese over at Lillian's.

Hazel went inside and saw her husband, Ethan Sinclair, a retired contractor, was already attaching dogs to their leashes and leashes to the hooks he'd welded to their golf cart.

Besides Ascot the spaniel and Fred the Alsatian, there were Fluffy the Great Dane, Spike the Pekinese, Harlow the Pomeranian, Angelina a Cocker Spaniel, Railroad the pug, Pacman the shar-pei, Sylvester and Nate, inseparable brothers, standard poodles, Alestra the chow and Alistair the chihuahua who bossed them all. Anything under fifteen pounds was attached to the golf cart Hazel drove; all the large dogs were attached to Ethan's cart. She helped him finish, grabbed her dog essentials bag and they all headed for the Fern Springs' dog park. Twelve dogs in all, earning them the title *master dog parents* in town as a joke. They fostered and found homes for dogs. However, some they simply couldn't part with, and they ended up staying.

Ethan headed up the local humane society. Right now, they had homes coming up for five of these dogs, but there were always other worthy dogs in need of rescue. Whenever the local dog shelter got a dog in they thought might be acceptable to Ethan, they called, generally a couple times a month. Right now, they were considering bringing a blue heeler into the mix. He needed gentling and training and would be able to be adopted out fairly quickly.

Once everyone was in place, Ethan climbed in, fired up Bertha the golf cart, and headed towards the park a mile away, dogs surrounding the cart, marching in time. His wife and her cart, Agnes, brought up the rear.

Hazel was a retired teacher. The kids she taught were now high schoolers or adults and they'd wave to her as she went by, surrounded by dogs, and she'd wave back. Max, the local cop, would watch them go by, shaking his head, not quite sure this was street legal, but they kept to side streets and obeyed the signs, so who was he to judge. Besides, she'd taught him years ago, and one of the things she said was obey all just laws and do the best with all the other ones. Once they arrived at the dog park, Ethan and Hazel took the dogs in one by one and let them run as a pack in the fenced two acres that was the park, walking along behind with scoops and depositing remains in the trash dispenser.

Back at her pink and white cape cod house, Lillian was going from window to window. Her husband, Samuel Hausted, used to work for and with Ethan and was an expert builder himself. One year for Lillian's birthday and his own sanity, he had connected two windows in the upstairs with one from the downstairs backrooms with fenced-in outdoor tunnels that ran along the outside back and sides of the house, attached firmly, with several small patios within them. When the weather was nice, the windows were opened and the cats all ran out to run and chase, sun themselves on the little platforms by the windows, and in general have a grand time going up down and around the house outdoors. The tunnels led to a partially enclosed cat pen on the roof, complete with cubby holes and platform perches. Lillian loved it, so did her animals, of which at last count there were Summer, Winter, Fall, Spring, and Minuet (Persians), Lily, Rose, and Daisy (Siamese), Josephus, Foxy, Fred, and Alberta (fosters, different colors, all with personality quirks that made them hard to place.).

Lilian raised Persians, Siamese, and occasionally Himalayans. She fostered other cats which were fixed and waiting for homes for the local humane shelter. The tunnels built around their house had earned her the sobriquet crazy cat lady. Lillian was a retired administrative assistant, having worked at the bank for 27 years, and having been replaced by Natalie Brown, a somewhat uppity woman who hated cats with a passion almost as virulent as her boss's dislike of dogs. They made a good pair. They ran a good bank. Animal lovers they were not.

Lillian opened the tunnels as soon as she saw the dogs leave for the park. The cats dashed out and she got to work super cleaning without their criticism. The Siamese especially hated the vacuum cleaner and the Swiffer mop gave them fits.

She had an old-fashioned pie safe she kept her baked goods in so no one unauthorized would sample them. It had a padlock on it, because Summer simply would stop trying. He had succeeded once in getting the doors open and ended up sitting on top of some warm pies while leisurely eating them. Blackberry juice does not come out of a cat's fur easily, nor does it come out of rugs, couches, or anything else he managed to run over before they caught him and put him in a carrier. He yowled for half an hour at the injustice while Samuel installed the locks. He still had a habit of sitting on the top of the pie safe when it was full of warm pies cooling.

Samuel Hausted was working in his shop this morning. In spite of all the cats, Lillian's house was always clean and organized and neat; there was always fresh baked bread and pies or cookies because she dearly loved her husband. Neighbor kids knew they could stop any time after school to help socialize the cats, and always find a welcome ear for their troubles, a couple cookies, and cold milk. She was the local secretary of the Humane Society now. Their two children were grown and had families of their own. Their life was full, furry, and happy.

Fern Springs was a pleasant little town in Ohio of about 6,000 residents, most of them having been born and raised there. Some of the kids went away to college and came back, some stayed away but always came home for holidays. The main industry was farming, with small farms polka dotted all around the town. There was an elementary and junior high school complex that had just been built and had all the fancy city people toys installed, electronic white boards and computers, a new gym. The high school kids were bused to the local district high school where they were joined by four other districts in a school of nearly a thousand students, between the vocational school and the regular high school. Everyone agreed their schools were simply the best and football games, basketball, soccer, and softball games were avidly followed and attended. The town had a nice sized grocery store, two gas stations (one at either end), a library, a police station, fire station, a couple medical clinics, and a few other small shops. There was no danger to anyone of something like a Walmart coming in and ruining all the mom-and-pop stores because all the land was in family farms that had gone back generations and which had children waiting to take them over, so there was simply no space for development to get a foothold. If you wanted to do that sort of shopping, you drove twenty miles to the nearest shopping mecca, somewhere up by Medina. Most folks didn't bother. They had a few eccentricities, but not more than any other small town. People made lifelong friends here, people helped each other out, and life was mostly good except for a couple small details.

First, Old Man Jameson and his brother Sam had decided to retire from their farms and had sold the land to Amish, of all things! There hadn't been any hereabouts up until now, and it still took some getting used to, seeing them come into town for supplies now and then. The townspeople were mostly friendly to them, but how could selling two farms of about thirteen hundred acres total have caused such an influx? It appeared there were several families of Amish and they seemed nice enough. They didn't send their children to school, which was odd. Jameson and his brother had never married and had no children to leave their farms to, so when they got up in years, and a good cash offer came, well, thank goodness they didn't sell to a developer but to good, sturdy, farm folk. Still, the Amish spoke an odd language, they didn't use electric in their homes, and those clothes!

Second, the ongoing feud between the five churches kept folks in gossip fodder for years. There had originally been one church, First Congregational on Main Street. Sometime around sixty years ago, there had been a disagreement on replacing the carpet and several families left and built a new church that had improved doctrines and blue carpeting throughout instead of the everlasting burgundy that the old church had. Forty years ago, a traveling Baptist preacher had come in, held a series of meetings, stole sheep from both folds, and now they had a Baptist church over on Vine Street. Fifteen years ago, the youth pastor at First Congregational had an affair with a lady in the congregation and they ran off together, which is a human enough problem, but that split the congregation into those who supported free love and those who didn't, so now there was a Unitarian church over on Garland Avenue. And finally, ten years ago, a Seventh-day Adventist family moved in, bought the local drug store, and had quietly raised a congregation and had a church building on a piece of land donated to them by a new member. It was a little out of town, in a nice grove of trees and they had a church school. They held occasional Revelation Seminars and had a reputation of being just a little odd, but nice enough folks. They worshipped on Saturday which was an inconvenience as it meant the drug store was closed on weekends, but they had an emergency number for the doctors only; if there was a specific medicine needed according to the doctor, the pharmacist would come in, get it, and deliver it personally.

So, the five churches did not always get along, but there were enough worship places you'd think the Amish would have found one of them to attend, but they seemed to wander from home to home having services a couple times a month. Still, they were quiet enough, no one really minded them, after all, putting up barns and continuing to use the land as farms kept the local economy stable, the land in good use, and everything seemed secure and peaceful. The Amish had put up a greenhouse and the residents of Fern Springs had been pleased to be able to get their spring plants at a reasonable price from local people; before, the grocer brought in plants from out of county and they were a bit pricey. They'd opened a bakery in one empty storefront and a fabric goods store in another, which also helped the local economy without hurting anyone.

Lillian and Hazel grew up together in Fern Springs. They both had met their husbands in community college and they both had raised their families here. They loved to read and together headed up the local library book club. Every Wednesday, they met at the library and talked over the latest book. They loved puzzles and hosted small get togethers at home in the winter for friends to come over, drink coffee and put together a puzzle while catching up on town gossip. Of late, they had been taking up reading spy novels and mysteries in the club; Agatha Christie and M.C. Beaton had them all fired up and longing for something between the Scottish Highlands and French detectives. They sort of wished for a mystery of their own, but really nothing happened in such a small farming community.

Within a couple hours, the house was vacuumed, dishes put away, breakfast cleaned up. The cats' food dishes and water dishes were filled and set up in the back room near the four automatic litter boxes. Lillian saw her friends return with their dogs and smiled. All seemed right in the world this morning. This afternoon was the library meeting and she had just enough time for the notes she wanted to make on the latest Officer Hamish McBeth tale.

Thank you for reading the trial run!

But in the meantime, as we complete the editing and design for the Furry Family book series, if you enjoy Christian fiction, you might enjoy the series I completed called *The Oberllyn Family Chronicles*. It traces the stories of a single family through three centuries in American history, past, present and future, with an eye on warning all those of us who love liberty and love the Lord what could happen to our freedoms if we don't guard them and pay attention to what is happening. The first book in the Series, <u>The Oberllyn's Overland</u>, deals with the family at the time of the Civil war and the Western Expansion. I'll be setting it into an omnibus soon, but the individual books are available right now. *Here's the first chapter....*

"Well, Ma, it's just about all I can stand," remarked Elijah Oberllyn as he stepped into the kitchen.

"What happened this time?" answered his wife, Elizabeth. She was busy rolling out the dough for homemade noodles on the wooden kitchen table. Behind her on the woodstove was bubbling a rich broth to cook them in. From the oven came the wonderful smell of peach pie baking, and warm bread stood on the counter, covered in tea towels. Elizabeth was short woman, with her long black hair, just starting to show grey, done up in a bun at the back of her neck, wearing a solid brown apron over a calico brown dress, and she looked capable of taking on the entire army and feeding it at once. Bustling as she rolled out the dough, she reminded you of a wren on a branch, swaying and hopping from task to task, chirping merrily in between.

"That neighbor Jacks," began her husband. "He's let his cattle get into my wheat again. He says he'll mend the fence but this time he said it was my fault because if I hadn't planted wheat, his cows wouldn't have been tempted, and he is talking about suing me for tempting his cows!"

His wife looked at him and finally said, "You're serious? He is going to try suing you for tempting cows?" She started to laugh out loud but hushed herself when she saw how angry her husband was. "It appears to me the only person to benefit from that would be the lawyers."

"He wants my field to add to his farm. He won't mend the fences on purpose. He's expecting me to do his fence. He's doing the same thing to our son. He offered him a pittance for his orchard, and when Noah wouldn't sell, he started rumors about him being half crazed since the church kicked him out during the great Disappointment and not being right so some of our own neighbors are questioning us for having our own services and I simply am not sure what to do. It's bad enough he picks on us but really, taking off after my son is just about all I can stand."

Elizabeth considered for a moment, then said quietly to her husband, "It's not much of a witness to be fighting with the neighbors. Joe wants to go to California to hunt for gold, but Catherine is not about to drop everything for a wild goose chase. Noah seems content here. I haven't spoken to Mary or Emily about it. I suppose we could consider moving but I hate the idea."

"We've lived here peaceably with our neighbors for years. It's only since those Jacks moved into their uncle's farm we've had trouble. Our land is fertile enough, but when Jacks heard we'd tried to buy his uncle's farm once, he took a dislike to us. And now look." Her husband poured himself a cup of coffee and sat down, blowing on it to cool it, then looking at is wife with a pensive expression on his face. "California is a right far piece to go," he started.

"Elijah! I was only giving you ideas from different members of the family, not saying I wanted to go." His wife turned with her hands on her hips, a distinctly displeased look on her face.

"It's a good idea and I might have to look into it. I don't want to be run out of town on a rail and that's just what that Jack's fellow is going to try and make happen. Besides, it's getting too crowded around here. It wasn't so bad before that train got put in. Now there are more people coming to buy land and settle in and it's just too crowded."

"Well, you need to pray about anything before you go off half-cocked," she said firmly. "Now go do your chores whilst I finish up supper."

Elijah went back to his barn and finished cleaning out stalls. His wife's jerseys would be up soon for milking. They'd cost him a pretty penny when he'd gotten them but had proven to be just what Ma's dairy business needed. They gave rich milk, it made wonderful cheese and butter, and their farm was getting known for its good fruit and cheese. Until that neighbor had moved here, everything had been going along fine. Joe had a good thought, though. Out west, there was plenty of land and it wasn't crowded. They could worship as they pleased on Saturday and not be accused of being Judaizers or crazy or anything else. He had two more children at home and there'd be no land to give them as a farm of their own if he couldn't buy up some land. When his son Nathaniel got married, it was a good thing he was a doctor who hadn't time to farm. The farm was just too divided up as it was, what with Emily and her brood, and

Catherine and David over by the creek running the small fruits part of the family business. Miriam's man Joe being a lawyer had helped; they'd just needed land for a house and little garden for themselves, no real farming involved. Noah and Mary had taken over the fruit orchard and were making a good go of it, and he and Elizabeth still had enough for him to raise the best horses and oxen in the county and keep mom's dairy running, but they needed more land. It just couldn't be divided anymore and there was Thomas and Johanna yet to be grown and have a part. He supposed Thomas could inherit their home but where would Joanna go? And that Jacks trying to force them to sell land to him they didn't have to spare, he and his dirty tricks. Hard to imagine what he'd try next. Maybe Joe had a good idea. *I believe I'll just visit the land office and find out about land west of here. It surely wouldn't be bad to have a look.*

He came out of the barn and stretched. His son Thomas came dashing up; that child never went anywhere at a walk, always running. "Pa, you got a letter."

"Oh? Thank you, son. Let's have a look." He took the letter from him. It was an official looking document from the US government. "Haven't seen one of these since well before you were born."

"Was that back when you and Ma lived in New York?"

"Yes, pretty much when you were a baby, before Grandpa died and we inherited the farm."

"Wonder what they want?"

"Whatever it is, your mother and I will deal with it. You're supposed to have seen to the goats."

"Done. You know the ma angora is going to give birth any day?" he grinned. "Can't wait to see them. I love the way the babies sprong around."

"Well, you keep a good eye on her."

Thomas hesitated. "Pa, I saw Mike Jacks over looking at Ma's sheep. He had this funny look on his face?"

"Funny like how?"

"He said his dad doesn't like sheep; they ruin the field. I told him it wasn't his field so not to worry about it. He said something under his breath and walked off. I don't like him much, Pa. I was hoping for a friend that would move in that I could do stuff with, but I don't think he likes me much."

"Don't worry about him. There are other folks to be with that don't cause such aggravation. Just be civil and leave him be."

"Yes, Pa. He made Johanna cry. Oh!" he covered his mouth.

"What?"

"I wasn't supposed to tell you."

"Stop right now. You don't keep secrets from me, ever. When was Johanna crying?"

"She went out to get the cows yesterday and Ellie Jacks was waiting and called her a cowgirl and teased her about her hair."

"What's wrong with her hair?"

"It's sort of red, I guess. And Johanna was crying when she helped with milking."

"I see. And you weren't supposed to tell me?"

"Johanna said we were having enough trouble with this family and God wouldn't want her complaining about it."

"I see. Well, you just let me handle this. Must be about time for supper, yes, there's Ma ringing the dinner bell. Let's go wash up."

Dad and Thomas washed up at the pump and went inside, hanging their hats by the door.

"That smell sure chirks a fellow up, ma. Can't wait to have some of your chicken and noodles."

Elizabeth smiled. "Johanna, would you mind getting the field tea I made? I put it in the springhouse to get cold." Johanna nodded and went out the door, coming back with a pitcher covered in a towel.

"Ma," she frowned. "I don't think we ought to use the tea."

"What's the matter?"

"Somebody's been in the spring house."

"Really? How do you know?"

"The cheeses are all on the floor and the milk's spilt." Ma and Pa rushed outside to the spring house where they found rounds of cheese scattered all over, the five-gallon milk cans flipped, polluting the spring run over. They looked around at the damage.

Ma shook her head. "I hate to think we'd have to put guards on our home, but this is outrageous."

"If we tell the sheriff," began Thomas.

"He'll say it could've been done by animals, that someone left the door open. There's no proof."

"Why don't we make a list of what's going on at least and ask him to watch out with us?" asked Ma.

"We can do that. Are the cheeses ruined?"

"The shelves are broken down, but the cheese ought to be fine. I may have to rewrap some."

"Let's see what we can do. Thomas – call Mick and Mike." Mike and Mick were the family mastiffs who spent most the time in the back field with the cattle. The dogs came to Thomas's call. "We'd best keep the dogs close to the yard or at least one of them here."

"Then who's going to protect the cattle from coyotes?" asked Thomas.

"It's not the four-legged ones I am worried about just now."

Thomas and Dad reset the shelves, and they helped Ma wipe off the wax coated cheeses and set them back. While they did that, Ma set the milk cans up and opened the overflow wide so the water could drain out and run clear. Finally, they stood up and went out. Dad shut the door to the spring house and set Mike by the door, telling him to stay. He took Mick to the barn and set him there and they went inside to eat.

The meal was a quiet one. Ma and Pa were tight-lipped and Thomas and Johanna were quiet as they passed food around.

"I don't care what they say. Johanna, you have got the prettiest hair in the world. It shines in the sun like gold and when you wear your green Sabbath dress I have the prettiest sister in the county."

Johanna looked surprised and her eyes welled up. "Thank you," she whispered.

"I agree with your brother. I am not quite sure why he said it but thank you for noticing," said Dad. Mom and Johanna just looked confused. Suddenly, there was a loud meow from out back.

"What on earth!" said Ma, getting up. She went out back where a strange collie dog had her pet cat up a tree. She took a switch and chased it off. The dog ran to the end of the driveway where Mike Jacks was watching.

"Lady, you'd better not hurt my dog," he yelled at her.

"Then keep him on your own land," she replied.

"Well, this is going to be our land when my dad gets done with you," he yelled back. "You'd better not let those sheep overgraze it."

Mom picked up a bigger switch and headed down the drive purposefully in his direction and he ran off. A passing wagon stopped.

"You all right, Mrs. Oberllyn?" said the farmer driving.

"I don't know, Zeb. We got neighbor problems. My spring house was attacked, they insult us and we just never did them any harm."

"I heard about some of that. Mr. Jacks was in the general store last week boasting he'd have your land soon. I don't know what he was talking about but I was coming to tell your husband if he was going to sell out, to call on me. I could use good fields like yours."

"I thank you, and I'll tell Elijah, but we have no interest in leaving our farm. It's been in the family for over a hundred years."

"Thought he might be blowing smoke. But still, keep me and my sons in mind. I'd rather buy from you than Jacks.

Oh, and best be careful. There's some weird rumors going around." Elijah was on the porch and waved to his neighbor.

"Rumors?"

"I'm sure they ain't true. You say howdy to Elijah for me."

"Thank you, Zeb. By the way, did he happen to say why he wanted my land?"

"He said it was the best land in the district and I have to agree with him. Your orchards make the best fruit, your cheese is wonderful, and you've always been real supportive of our community. Shame to have you leave."

"Aren't planning on leaving."

"I hope not. Well, I best be getting home. You remember my offer."

Ma went to the back where Thomas had climbed the tree and gotten her Maine coon cat down. He jumped into her arms. "There, there, dear. I'm sorry he flustered you so. Shh, now. Shhh."

"Mom, why do they hate us?"

"I have no idea." They went inside. "We've never had this much trouble."

"Mom, did you know Jacks have got slaves?"

"What?"

"They have three of them. I saw them out working his field. And Mr. Jacks carries a whip."

"I see. Well, the good Lord never wanted slavery. We earn our needs by the works of our hands, not the sweat of others. Let's try to finish supper. It's most likely all cold by now, but even cold, your ma's food is good.."

About the Author:

J. Traveler Pelton was born in West Virginia in the last century. She served as Nation's Mother for her tribe, for six years. She is wife to Dan (45 years!), mother of six adults, a grandmother of eight, a Clinically Licensed Independent Social Worker with Supervisory Status, at present in private practice, a retired adjunct professor of social work at her local university and an insatiable reader. She is a cancer survivor. Traveler avidly studies science and technology, fascinated by the inventiveness of people. She is quick to draw parallels in different fields and weave stories around them. Traveler is a fabric artist and her most enjoyable time is spent spinning yarn while spinning yarns for the grandkids.

You can reach Traveler at her website:
travelerpelton.com

Or like us and share us on **Facebook at Traveler Pelton**

Or write to her by **snail mail** at
Springhaven Croft
212 Sychar Rd.
Mt. Vernon, OH 43050

<u>She loves to hear from her readers!</u>

All our books are available on Amazon as both eBook and print copy, Kindle unlimited as free downloads

<u>**We'd love it if you'd leave us a review! It helps others find our books.**</u>

God bless and see you in our next travels together!

Your Attention Please!!!!

<u>Would you like to join the team at Potpourri Books?</u>

Traveler is <u>always</u> looking for responsible beta readers for her new books. A beta reader gets a prepublication copy of all new books, <u>free of charge</u> in exchange for an honest review written on Amazon, and a short email letting her know of any glitches you may have found that got past the editor, any suggestions you may have, and your opinion of the book. What else do you get out of it?

A beta reader gets:
A free download of one of her already published books
and
as soon as your review of that book gets placed on
Amazon,
free downloads of her already published works: for each review, you get a free book.
And
A free copy pre-publication copy of all new books…
And
Other neat freebies as they come, from bookmarks to stickers to posters to pens to neat things I find to send out to my betas-
Interested?
Contact Traveler at
travelerpelton@gmail.com for more info…

We would love to add you to the team!

Dear Lord,
Give me a few friends
who will love me for what I am,
and keep ever burning
before my vagrant steps
the kindly light of hope...
And though I come not within sight
of the castle of my dreams,
teach me to be thankful for life,
and for time's olden memories
that are good and sweet.
And may the evening's twilight
find me gentle still.

Old Celtic blessing….

I've seen better days, but I've also seen worse.
I don't have everything that I want, but I do have all I need.
I woke up with some aches and pains, but I woke up.
My life may not be perfect, but I am blessed."
Anonymous

Until you join me on another journey, may you be blessed as well!

www.ingramcontent.com/pod-product-compliance
Lightning Source LLC
Chambersburg PA
CBHW071938150726
47999CB00001B/253